FALSE COLOURS

Recent Titles by Judith Saxton from Severn House

THE LOVE GIFT
THE SILKEN THREAD
WATERLOO SUNSET
THE WINYARD FORTUNE

FALSE COLOURS

Judith Saxton

This title first published in Great Britain 2001 by
SEVERN HOUSE PUBLISHERS LTD of
9–15 High Street, Sutton, Surrey SM1 1DF,
complete with new Introduction from the author.
Originally published 1982 by Hamlyn Paperbacks
under the title *Masquerade* and pseudonym *Jenny Felix.*
This title first published in the USA 2002 by
SEVERN HOUSE PUBLISHERS INC of
595 Madison Avenue, New York, N.Y. 10022.

British Library Cataloguing in Publication Data

Saxton, Judith, 1936-
  False colours
  I. Title
  823.9'14 [F]

  ISBN 0-7278-5791-6

Printed and bound in Great Britain by
MPG Books Ltd., Bodmin, Cornwall.

Introduction

Twenty years ago, I was writing my first family saga for Hamlyn paperbacks, when my editor told me that the firm was starting a romance list. To quote her, "The stories must be squeaky clean". I was keen to have a go and having just read a book on distant water trawling I decided to put my heroine aboard such a vessel.

Little did I dream how difficult the setting would be! No strolls on the dark deck, no plunges into a crystal ocean, not even a visit to a cinema or a meal in a restaurant. Danger and death await anyone who forgets for one second that the seas at the top of the world are your enemy, but I revelled in the strangeness of the Arctic and enjoyed every minute of writing the book.

And of course, the trawler and her cargo got safe to port - and I decided to make the next book easier!

1

It was an ice-cold night. The street lights which lit the docks wore haloes of mist and seemed to waver in the wind. Stars and moon were blacked out by the cloud over and the townfolk slept. It would be hours before ordinary people awoke to a new day.

With her feet numb inside her Wellington boots despite two pairs of socks, and her chilled fingers dug deep into the pockets of her duffle coat, Frances Louisa Willoughby flinched as the wind cut across the open dockyard but continued doggedly crossing towards the quayside. She had not journeyed here by bus, train and now on foot, to turn back because it was cold and dark! She was going to find Trevor and tell him that she had taken his advice after all; she had left home.

Only a few days before, she and Trevor had quarrelled because of her stubborn refusal to leave Aunt Delia, the farm and her cousins.

'You're stupid, Frankie.' Trevor had said severely. 'They don't give a damn about you! You work like a lad in the cowsheds and stables, you dance attendance on your spoilt cousins—why don't you get away? Go to London, or Manchester. Come to me, for that matter, I'd see you were all right.'

'I have to work, to make up to Aunt Delia for taking me in after my parents were killed,' Frankie pointed out defensively. 'And then there's Nip. But I will leave one day, or I would if I knew what I could do, apart from farmwork. I can't do shorthand, or type, I was rotten at maths at school. Go on, if you're so clever, what could I do?'

'A thousand things! You could...Damn it, you could...' he had stuttered to a stop, as aware as she that careers in the north-east of England at a time of recession were not easy to come by. 'Look, if you came to the port I sail from I could get you work as...as a waitress, at first. You could lodge with Mrs. Cheetham. She may be a stupid, avaricious old bag, but she wouldn't let you starve, not if she knew you were my girl! That would be just for now, of course. When my present tour ends, we could make proper arrangements.'

'Well, perhaps next time you're home...'

'All right, Frankie, stay here, be a Cinderella. But don't expect any sympathy from me!'

He had stormed out of the house and she had gone up to her bedroom to have a good cry, and then she tried to put the whole quarrel out of her mind.

She might have succeeded, might have remained with Aunt Delia, if Nip had not been killed.

Nip was a scrawny mongrel with a good deal of terrier somewhere in his mixed ancestry. He was obedient only to Frankie, and he loved her with all his soul. She had watched the whole thing from her bedroom window, seen her cousin Pat drive in, hoot impatiently at the hens, then back the Rover incredibly fast into the big barn which served as a garage. Nip had been in the barn, had run towards the car. Her mind shuddered away from the recollection.

Even then she might have stayed, nursing her grief, but for Uncle Arthur ringing Aunt Delia when she was in the downstairs cloakroom trying to tidy up the coats and scarves which always seemed to end up on the floor.

'Arthur? A weekend in London? How kind you are, such a good brother to me, we'd adore to come. The girls will be ecstatic, especially Pat. She ran over that wretched mongrel of Frankie's, it upset her dreadfully, so she needs cheering up.' There was a pause, during which Uncle Arthur's deep voice could be faintly heard, then Aunt Delia spoke again. 'Frankie? Oh, she's very hard, you know. She didn't shed a tear. As for London, she wouldn't be interested. But in any case, she couldn't possibly come. *Someone* has to keep an eye on the farm!'

It had been the final straw. To dismiss her grief, her very real anguish, to refuse her even the chance of a trip to London, yet never to acknowledge her usefulness by saying she was really needed on the farm, that the workers trusted her.

There and then, Frankie put on her rubber boots with the jeans and sweater she was already wearing. She added the thick duffle coat and walked calmly past her aunt, still gushing into the telephone, across the farmyard, down the lane and away from Hightops Farm and the Smithson family for ever.

The warmth of her fury kept her glowing throughout the train journey, but to arrive anywhere at ten o'clock on a freezing January night is depressing, and perhaps a port is the most depressing of all. Only the thought of Trevor's praise and pleasure when he saw her, the warm approval on his face, kept her from shedding a few tears and casting herself on the mercy of the local police. As it was, she told herself severely that it was always darkest before dawn, that a new life was opening up before her, and that she must make her way straight to the docks.

Her arrival there was daunting. They covered acres and acres of ground and the signs and indications which were written over the place might have been in Dutch for all they meant to her. But, in the nick of time, she remembered one thing Trevor had said. 'We sail at dawn, when the tide's right. No one can leave harbour just when they please, you know. So we'll steam out through the lock gates when morning's coming up.'

This meant that she must look for signs of imminent departure and at last she found them. A dock where a few people stood about, muffled to the eyebrows, and small ships obviously ready to sail. She made her way across the gleaming tarmac to stand in the slight shelter of a pile of boxes smelling strongly of fish. There was a man with papers in his hand, wearing a woollen cap pulled down over his eyes and a long overcoat with the collar turned up. He was shuffling up and down beside one of the ships, shouting 'Three to come!' and occasionally glancing up at the bridge above him. There, behind the glass of the bridge, Frankie could see that men were working, moving restlessly back and forth, glancing out at the quay as if they were waiting for something. Or someone.

She was about to move on when the man in the long overcoat moved and she saw the name of the ship. It was partly obscured by shadow, but she could make out most of it.... *tic Glow,* it read, and Frankie smiled to herself. She had done it! Trevor's ship was the *Atlantic Glow;* now all she had to do was to find Trevor and everything would be all

11

right. Even if there was only time for him to lend her some money and scribble a note of introduction to his landlady, that would be sufficient. The only thought she could not face was being stranded here, penniless, whilst his ship stole away on the dawn tide with Trevor aboard, never even knowing she was here!

She moved towards the ship and above her, she heard the bridge door open. Someone was coming out! It must be an officer, or the captain. Suppose it was Trevor!

'Two to come...Two to come...' the mo notonous voice of the man with the list had a plaintive note in it. Frankie guessed that he was marking off the crew as they arrived and wondered if Trevor was still not aboard. But it seemed unlikely; discipline on a merchantman might be nothing like discipline in the Royal Navy, but nevertheless, Trevor had instructed her, one obeyed instantly. No, Trevor must be aboard now, carrying out his duties. If only...

'Hey! You there! The lad in the duffle coat!'

The voice was deep and carrying and came from the ship. Frankie glanced up to the deck to see a tall man, dark hair flopping over his brow and a duffle coat on, apparently addressing someone near her. She glanced round. She was standing quite alone. She looked up at the man again and saw his dark eyes staring impatiently down at her.

'Yes-yes? S-sir? Were you talking to me?'

"Who else? D'you want a berth?'

'What?'

The man came to the rail and beckoned. She walked slowly closer, eyes wide and black in the faint light.

'Do you want a berth?' The man said the words slowly and distinctly, but the impatience in his voice was so obvious that she almost flinched. 'I'm two men short, and you looked as if you might be after a berth, so...'

'A berth?'

The man clenched his hands into fists and smote them against the rail.

'Yes, a berth! It's a job, lad, a job! Pays well, too. Galley boy. Look, if you weren't hoping for a berth whatever are you doing here at this time of night?'

There was enough suspicion in his voice to make up Frankie's mind for her.

'Yessir! I want a berth!'

But now, having had the answer he obviously expected, it seemed he felt some qualms. He came slowly down the short gangplank until he stood scarcely a foot from her. He was very tall, and the breadth of his shoulders made him seem formidable. Frankie swallowed.

'You're very slight. D'you think you can stand up to the voyage? And what about your parents? We could radio them from the ship,

13

but if they refuse permission...How old are you? What's your name? Address?'

'I'm sixteen, sir. Frankie Willoughby of Randall Street, and my p-parents won't mind. They know I'm looking for a berth.'

Later, she marvelled at her own quickness. She had given the address of the house where Trevor lodged, and until the words were out she would have denied even *knowing* the address!

'All right, we'll take a chance on you. Hawkins, did you get that?' He turned to the man in the long overcoat. 'Change the last name to Frank Willoughby of Randall Street. And if young Spud turns up, tell him we've sailed without him.'

He checked the list in the man's hand, nodded curt approval, then jerked his head towards the ship.

'Get aboard, youngster. We'll give Meadowes a few more minutes before we start preparing to sail. Can you find the galley?'

He followed her aboard and for a moment, Frankie hesitated. What had she done? But it was not too late, she could confess, tell him that she only wanted to get aboard to look for Trevor!

'What the devil are you standing there for? Get below!' A hard hand propelled her down a short flight of stairs. 'If you're worried about bad-weather gear, don't. It's kept aboard and

Spud's stuff will fit you. Go to the galley!'

He made as if to follow her and her reso-lution fled. She hurried down the short corridor and heard him chuckle behind her, then the sound of his boots as he returned to the rail or the bridge, she could not tell which. She found the galley simply by the smell of cooking, but hesitated outside the door. Then she pushed it open and entered. I'm not afraid of that captain, she told herself firmly, but it might be better not to annoy him right now. The skipper, Trevor had impressed upon her, was a mighty being, a demi-god, whose word was law and who could have you practically flogged at the mast head if you annoyed him.

The galley was crowded and crammed with cooking utensils, food and crockery. A huge negro was stoking the galley fire, on which a pot of coffee bubbled and steamed invitingly. Frankie swallowed. It had been many hours since she had last eaten or drunk anything at all and the coffee smelt delicious.

The cook did not turn as she entered the room but said in a lazy drawl: 'Swing for you I will one of these days, Spuddy-boy! Git into working clothes now!'

'I-I'm not Spud. I'm Frankie.'

He swung round at that, a huge grin splitting his face.

'Frankie! There's foolish I am, thinking you were Spud.' He offered a gigantic paw. 'I'm

Taffy Evans, from Cardiff. Nice to meet you. Skipper signed you on because Spud's not turned up?'

'Yes. I suppose so. He offered me a berth, and...'

'Aye. Well, get you down to Spud's cabin, and put on working togs, now.' He glanced down at her feet. 'Keep them boots on. Spud 'ad feet like an elephant, I doubt his boots 'ud fit. You'll bunk aft.'

Frankie nodded nervously, and turned quickly out of the galley. From the noises coming from the deck above, she had better get off, and not bother about fore and aft! She was making her way to the stairs which led on to the deck when someone clattered down them, someone in a duffle coat and seaboots, with a tartan bag swinging from one hand. In the brightly lit interior of the ship she could see at a glance that it was not Trevor, but it was a cheerful young man with an open countenance who grinned at her before pushing her down the narrow corridor.

'Skipper said to show you your cabin. You're galley, ain't you? I'm Jammy Tolbooth, deck 'and. Spud and me's the youngest—was, I should say—now it's you and me. You berth by me, right near all the nobs. Single berths too, height of luxury. Here we are!'

'But...but...but...' stammered Frankie,

16

as the ship seemed to heave convulsively beneath her feet. 'But...but...'

'But me no buts matey,' advised Jammy Tolbooth in a cheerful cockney accent. 'We're leaving port and you'd best get yourself sorted and back to the galley double quick. Skip'll expect a bloody good breakfast on the table soon's we're clear of the lanes. Git moving!'

He pushed her through a narrow doorway, indicating the tiny slip of a cabin with a wave of his hand.

'Where are Spud's working things?' Frankie said doubtfully, realising that her new benefactor did not intend to leave her just standing there. 'I can't see anything.'

She could see only a narrow bunk, a shelf above it, what looked like empty bookshelves along the foot and a leather covered wall bench.

'Under the bunk,' Jammy said briefly. 'Come on, skip said I was to see you right and go back on deck.' He reached under the bunk and produced a couple of cardboard boxes. 'Sling your duffle on the 'ook and strip off, then put these on.' He held up a scruffy pair of corduroy trousers and a dingy brown pullover. 'And a pinny, ducky!'

The 'pinny' was a vast apron made of some sort of American cloth and, with Jammy's eyes upon her, Frankie took off her duffle

17

coat, then her dark blue sweater and jeans. Standing awkwardly on the tilting deck in a loose white shirt many sizes too large for her which she had inherited from an uncle, she could only be grateful for its multitudinous folds and for her own small breasts. There was a spotted mirror above the bunk and even in her own eyes, it could have been a woebegone little lad who stood there, trying to get the corduroy trousers on whilst the movements of the ship seemed to baulk him at every turn!

When she left the cabin at last, she wore the brown pullover, which almost reached her knees, and the corduroys, but not Spud's enormous boots.

'Your own'll do fine,' Jammy encouraged, his impatience clear. 'Git a move on, I want to wave to Lucy.' Without any further explanations he left her, bounding up the stairs to the deck.

Frankie returned to the galley, noticing that the smell of coffee no longer seemed quite so enticing. In fact, the heat of the little room was making her head swim, and there was a heaviness on the back of her neck as though a large hot hand was trying to press her down towards the floor.

'Hi, Frankie. Pass me that bacon, will you? And pour yourself a cuppa coffee. You don't want to work on an empty stomach!'

The very words made Frankie's stomach churn but she sat down on the stool which the cook had indicated and reached for the pot. The coffee, hot and sweet, reached her stomach in one long, glorious swoop—and left it in much the same manner. Taffy yelled and shoved a bowl under her nose in the nick of time, shaking with ill-concealed amusement.

'Happens to us all, boyo. Git on deck, git some air!'

Clutching her mouth, Frankie bolted.

She reached the deck and stood by the rail for a moment, taking deep breaths of the cold, salty air. Gulls, ignoring her, were perched like beads on a necklace, all along the rail. Two figures in oilskins were scurrying about to her right, another two figures lounged at their ease on her left. She turned and looked up towards the bridge. The captain, catching her eye, grinned. It was not a sympathetic grin, but how could he guess at her inner anguish?

Frankie turned back to the rail and the last of the coffee plummeted to its death in the cold North Sea. Where, oh where, was Trevor?

For two whole days, Frankie walked the ship like a zombie, careless of everything but her agonies. She did her best to help Taffy, but most of the time what he wanted was beyond her. No one in the world, she was convinced, had ever vomited so much or so often. By the end of the first night aboard she urgently wanted to die. Trevor's whereabouts no longer mattered. Trevor himself might have appeared at the end of her bunk and she would not have turned a hair. In fact, when the mate took pity on her on the second day and accompanied her on to the bridge to see the captain, she could not even bring herself to thank him. She just stood where he had propped her and longed for death.

'Skip, I've never seen a lad so ill before, and I've seen plenty. Got anything which would help?'

That was the mate, his voice concerned.

'I've got some stuff.' The captain's voice was amused and Frankie lifted her sagging lids to give him an embittered glare. How could anyone laugh over another's misery! He looked the picture of health, standing over her with the dark hair flopping over his forehead and his eyes narrowing with concentration as he poured a dose of something brown and evil-smelling from a bottle into a small glass. 'Come on, lad, open your mouth!'

Frankie tightened her lips. Everything made her sick, even water, so it was unlikely that the medicine would stay down long enough to do any good.

Before she had realised what he intended

to do, she was clamped against his shoulder, one hand forced her chin up, he opened her mouth as she had so often seen a vet open a reluctant animal's, and the glass with its foul smelling contents was clinking against her teeth.

'Down the hatch!' He tilted the glass and she gasped, choked and swallowed and then, shamingly, felt tears burn in her eyes and slide down her cheeks. 'There, you'll soon be fit to work again.' He released her and gave her a shove towards the door. 'Go to your cabin and sleep it off. You'll be fighting fit when you wake.'

She just managed one last glare, then she swayed and staggered to her berth. She slumped on to the bunk fully clothed, intending to strip down to her shirt, to take her boots off...and knew no more. For the first time since she had come aboard, sleep claimed her.

She awoke a different person. New-born, she thought drowsily, staring up at the swaying light fixture above her head. Her stomach was a hollow void, but she felt perfectly well, if hungry. She climbed out of her bunk and stood up cautiously, but the tilt of the floor beneath her feet, the surge of the ship, worried her not at all. Whatever she might think of the heartless, detestable man, the captain's medicine seemed to have done the trick.

21

As soon as she was washed and dressed, she made her way to the galley. Today, she felt it in her bones, she would find Trevor!

'Morning, Frankie. Better? There, folk never die of seasickness, they just think they're going to! You'll be all right now, they always are. Can you take this food to the officers now, boyo?'

There was a laden tray on the table and Frankie picked it up, staggering a little under the weight.

'Of course. Where do they eat?'

'I didn't take you in there, did I? So ill you were! Follow me!'

With bumping heart, Frankie followed. She was taking the officers their breakfast, she could see the sizzling rashers of bacon protruding from beneath one of the steel food covers. At last she could not fail to see Trevor! In her excitement it never occurred to her that there might be difficulties ahead when Trevor found his breakfast being served to him by his childhood sweetheart!

But in the officers' cabin a crushing disappointment awaited her. Five men sat round the table, the skipper, the mate and three other men Frankie had not seen before. But none of them was Trevor.

On the way back to the galley she questioned Taffy.

'Where were the other officers, Taffy? Were they on watch or something?'

Tally stopped short just outside the galley door to tap a thermometer which hung there, but at her question he turned towards her, eyes white-rimmed with surprise.

'Them *are* the officers, lad. Why, what's up?'

For Frankie was staring at the thermometer—the legend traced on it was all too clear—*Arctic Glow!*

'Taffy! What ship is this?'

The cook took the question as a joke and laughed, continuing on into the galley.

'I'm not drunk so early in the day, Frankie! She's the E.470 *Arctic Glow,* bound for the fishing grounds in the far north. Why?'

The deck seemed to tilt nightmarishly beneath Frankie's feet. She staggered, clutching at the kitchen table for support.

'My God! A fishing boat?'

'She's a trawler. Why? Don't say you thought you was aboard the Queen Elizabeth, laddie!'

Afterwards, Frankie thought she must have made some suitable remark because Taffy nodded and laughed and reached for a pan of potatoes. But Frankie's mind was whirling. She was aboard the wrong ship, going in the wrong direction, and it was absolutely vital that she tell someone and get

23

the mistake sorted out. For a moment she could think of nothing but her predicament and had to jerk herself out of her daze when Taffy told her to clear the mess-deck.

'Then we'll have ours. Make it quick, boyo.'

By the time she had cleared away the deck-hands' meal and eaten her own breakfast, Frankie knew there was only one course open to her. She must tell the skipper, and then he could turn around and take her back to port. He would probably be very cross with her, but it wouldn't hurt him to lose a couple of days!

So when Taffy told her to clear the officers' table she made for the door, determined this time to tell the skipper everything.

Down in the officers' cabin the skipper was alone, standing by the table moodily reading a long sheet of paper and ticking it with a biro at intervals. Of the other officers there was no sign. Frankie cleared her throat.

'Er...Skipper?'

Without looking up, he nodded towards the table.

'You can clear.'

'Oh. Th-thank you.'

She glanced at him as she moved around the table, filling her tray with the used dishes and cutlery. He was a big man, his lean face made harsh, at the moment, by a scowl which brought the dark brows close over his high-bridged nose. He was wearing a thick, white fisherman's jersey with a roll collar which met his chin and dark trousers pushed into the massive seaboots which all the men seemed to favour. He looked efficient and dangerous; rather like a buccaneer—she could almost see his hand going to the sword which might have hung at his side!

She was still smiling at the thought when, as if sensing her scrutiny, he looked up.

'What's the matter? Not wanting to change your mind?'

She hesitated. Dare she tell him?

'It i-isn't exactly...'

He cut across her stammered reply, his own voice crisp and decisive.

'Good. Because no one changes their mind aboard my ship! Get a move on with those things, or you'll still be clearing in here when Taff comes in to lay for lunch!'

Frankie grabbed nervously at the sugar basin. No, it was not the moment to tell him anything. He was scowling down at the sheet of paper again, then the biro came into play as he scored through a line. Ruthlessly, Frankie bit her lip and piled the last dishes on to the tray and then, maliciously almost, the ship lurched as she met a heavy sea head-on.

The skipper swayed lightly on the balls of his feet, hardly seeming to notice the roll of the ship, and Frankie tried to emulate him.

But the tray had other ideas. It tilted, Frankie grabbed and six plates and a sugar basin met the floor with a tinkling crash.

'Young fool! You're supposed to make two journeys.'

Frankie muttered an apology, stood the tray down and knelt on the floor, trying to gather all the broken china into a neat heap. Even as she went to rise, however, the ship lurched and plunged again and she slid across the cabin floor and struck her head a resounding blow on the door panel.

For a moment she literally saw stars. Then she felt hands lift her to her feet and stand her down, none too gently. She was leaning against the skipper's chest, still dazed, whilst his hands ran lightly but firmly over her limbs.

'No bones broken. Just a knock on the head and some bruising round the ribs, and...'

The hand which had been gently exploring her ribs moved upward and before she could pull away, it was on her breast—and off again, as if she were red-hot.

She opened her eyes and blinked into the dark face above her own. He was staring down at her as if he could not believe his eyes.

'You're a *girl!* God Almighty, a woman aboard my ship when we're heading for the arctic!' He stood back from her so quickly that she staggered and, glancing up at him, she saw fury had replaced the incredulity in his eyes. 'You bloody little fool, what the devil do you mean by it?' He grabbed her shoulders and shook her until the soft, golden-brown hair fell blindingly across her eyes, hiding the tears in them, though he could still see her soft, trembling mouth. 'Which of the men brought you aboard? Damn it, I'll have him blacked from every trawler in every fleet afloat! And as for you...' He shook her again, harder if anything. 'You cheap little tart! Who brought you aboard?'

'N-no one. Honestly, I s-swear it. I c-came aboard because you offered me a berth, you know you did!'

He released her and stepped back. She pushed the hair out of her eyes and wiped her tear-stained cheeks with both hands. She knew she must not show her fear.

'By God, you're right! I remember thinking when I saw you on the quay that you were lurking there as if...' he caught her shoulders again, bringing her close to him, making. her gasp with pain as his fingers dug into her small, fragile bones. 'What's your game? Come on, the truth now!'

The pain and shock of the blow on the head and the shaking were receding. She glared up at him, trying to show her contempt.

27

'I don't have a game! Let me go, I'm not one of your crew! I came aboard to find a friend, I meant to leave, only...'

'Only you left it too late! Well, my pretty, you *are* one of my crew whether you like it or not, and you'll stay one of my crew what's more.' He looked at her white face, with the bruise already beginning to show on her forehead where she had struck the door and his expression softened a little. 'Sit down. There's some coffee left in the pot, I'll pour us both a cup. We need it.'

She sat weakly on a chair and watched him pour the strong, black coffee. He sweetened it lavishly, then looked up at her and, for the first time since he had discovered her secret, smiled at her. It changed him; she could glimpse a man behind the skipper, a man who could be kind, perhaps even tender. Then the smile was gone and the harsh, ruthless look was back.

'Drink that.' He handed her a cup of coffee, then sat down in the chair opposite her own. 'I suppose you thought that I'd radio back to port and turn round and take you home. But I shan't.'

She knew her apprehension must show on her face but tried to sound nonchalent.

'You won't? Why not?'

'Because we're nearly three days out, my child, and that means we'd lose six days going home and then returning to our present position, and we're still two days from the fishing grounds. This trip must succeed. I won't have you ruining it.'

'Then what will you do with me?'

She had meant the question to sound cool, off-hand, but she was mortified to hear the words come out in a sort of breathless squeak. To make up for it she raised her brows haughtily, but he was not even looking at her.

'You'll stay aboard and remain a boy. The chances of anyone else discovering your secret are pretty remote but if they do find out, you'll get no mercy from me. I've superstitious men aboard who'd sooner carry plague than a woman! And some of the younger ones would find a use for you which wouldn't improve their performance at the trawl.' He allowed his glance to flicker insultingly over her, as if he could see through the rough clothing to the secrets of her naked body beneath it. 'So you must remain a boy for the rest of the trip. Is that clear?'

Frankie, scarlet blooming hotly in her cheeks, nodded. The captain stood up, then stretched out a hand to help her to her feet and, once she was standing, took her chin in his hand and forced her face up until her eyes met his. Still holding her chin, he pulled her close. She tightened her lips, trying to jerk herself free, but his mouth descended on hers.

He kissed her strongly, fiercely, and she knew he could feel the hammering of her heart, the breath coming short in her throat, and felt as humiliated by her weakness as she was sure he intended.

He released her at last, breathing hard, looking down into her ashamed eyes with mocking scorn.

'Behave yourself, and remain a boy. Or you know what I'll do.'

She fled from him then, forgetting the tray, the broken china, everything. Because his message was insultingly clear. If she did not keep her secret, she would be the captain's whore by the time they made port once more.

2

'**F**inished 'ave you, Frankie? Take the slops out, then.'

Frankie had been mopping down the long wooden table which occupied the centre of the galley but now she nodded to Taffy and got her duffle coat down off the hook behind the door. She guessed that it would be cold outside, though they were still a day's steaming from the fishing grounds where they would shoot the trawl for the first time this trip. She put the coat on then opened the door, to be stopped in her tracks by Taffy's voice.

'What are you doing, boyo? You go up there now without something round your mouth and you won't be singing no songs! Ice crystals in the lungs kill!'

Frankie turned to stare. Was he teasing her? But the black, shiny face was solemn. She turned back into the galley.

'What should I do, then?'

'See that brown muffler? Wrap it right around the lower half of your face, nose and all. And put on them mittens.'

Without another word, Frankie did as she

was bidden. Only when she was completely wrapped with only her eyes showing did she pick up the heavy bucket of kitchen refuse and leave the galley.

Outside, the cold hit her. It was light still, but the sky lowered, heavy with the threat of snow, and the wind was keen. The small strip of her face still exposed felt as though it had been doused in cold water. She gripped the bucket more tightly, then staggered across the deck to heave the contents over the rail. A muffled roar from behind her made her pause. With some difficulty, she swung round to see who was calling.

'What's the matter? It's only the kitchen rubbish.'

A large figure in duffle coat and seaboots loomed up beside her. She could tell by the moth-eaten, Russian-style hat that it was Spick, one of the deckhands. He took the bucket from her firmly.

'Not this side, you young fool! D'you want to spend the rest of the day cleaning muck off the ship? Always chuck stuff overboard so the wind takes it away and don't carry it inboard. See?'

She crossed the deck meekly in his wake and watched as, effortlessly, he lifted the bucket shoulder-high and cascaded its contents over the side.

'I see. Thanks very much, Spick.'

He grunted.

'Just remember it. Making a duff down in the galley?'

She understood the men's preoccupation with food, for until they reached the fishing grounds they had little else to think about, and when they were fishing, Taffy told her, the work was so cruelly hard, the conditions so bitter, that good food was essential.

'Well, not a duff. Apple pudding, I think. I've peeled pounds and pounds of Bramleys, anyway.'

He grinned. She could tell only by the wrinkles which appeared round his eyes, for he was as muffled as she.

'Fine. Skip's wanting you.'

Frankie's heart skipped a beat. It would be the first time she had encountered the captain since their confrontation in his cabin the previous day.

'Oh? How do you know? What have I done?'

Spick grinned and cuffed her in what was meant to be a friendly fashion. Frankie staggered.

'He's in the bridge, when I looked up he pointed at you and then beckoned. As for what you've done, don't worry. It's new brooms sweeping clean, kiddo! A chap who takes command at the last minute wants everything right.'

'Oh, I didn't know he was new. Thanks for telling me.'

Frankie made her way to the bridge, the

empty bucket swinging at her side. That, she thought ruefully, explained a lot. No doubt when he had been waiting for the man called Meadowes he had been half hoping, half dreading, that he might have to step into the skipper's shoes. Now that he had, of course, he would be completely determined to make the voyage a success. No wonder he had been so furious at the mere suggestion that they might turn back, to take her home to Grimsby! It just went to show that you should never judge people's actions until you knew exactly why they had made them. Perhaps he was not so hard after all!

She stepped into the warmth and brightness of the bridge and glanced across at the skipper. Immediately, all her sympathy with his position receded. His mouth was set grimly, his grey eyes bleak.

'Boy! Did I see you emptying slops over the weather side?'

Frankie felt her cheeks begin to burn underneath the muffler. She dragged it clear so that she could speak properly.

'No you did not! Well, I might have, but Spick...'

'Saved your bacon!' He glanced round the bridge, which was empty, save for themselves. 'Are you all right?'

She could not delude herself that he cared what the answer was, but she nodded dumbly.

34

'No trouble? Nobody suspicious? No suggestions on the mess deck that they play strip poker instead of brag?'

Frankie scowled, but remained silent.

'What, sulking?' He walked over to her, standing so close that she could smell the clean, male smell of his skin, the faint oiliness of the shetland wool sweater that he wore. He put out a hand and tilted her chin. Remembering the last occasion when he had touched her she shrank back but he followed her up, his eyes mocking. 'Nothing to say? You're quite safe in here, you know. The intercom's switched off, there's no one on deck looking in this direction at the moment. If you've got troubles, tell me now and I'll see...'

She swallowed. If only he would move back a little! Yet there was no need to fear him, not on the bridge, with the deckhands liable to glance up at any moment. But she could not forget his threat and spoke quietly, the words almost tumbling over each other.

'Trouble, sir? No, honestly, everything's fine. I don't th-think anyone suspects... it's the last thing which... which...'

He cut across her stammered explanation without haste.

'Good. Off with you, then.' He watched her until she reached the door, then added cryptically: 'Report to me daily, on the bridge. Understand?'

She said: 'Aye aye, sir,' without glancing round, and slipped out of the door, thankfully shutting it behind her. Phew! For some reason, being alone with him was every bit as frightening and disconcerting as being alone with a hungry tiger! As for the men, she had spoken no more than the truth when she had said no one suspected the truth about her. They treated her as they would have treated any young lad; there was camaradie when they thought about it, a hint of violence in the hand which jerked her to her feet when she slipped or hurried her through a doorway. Impatience sometimes, indifference often, but not a breath of suspicion.

Returning to the galley, she stood the bucket down by the sink and began to take off her outer clothing. Taffy, stirring a stew over the stove, glanced across at her.

'You've been gone a whiles, Frankie. What kept you?'

Frankie, hanging her coat and muffler back on the hook, grimaced.

'The captain. He saw me going to throw stuff out into the wind and hauled me over the coals. Only he needn't have, because Spick grabbed the bucket off me before I'd emptied anything!'

Taffy chuckled.

'Worse sin a galley boy can commit, that. Unless you throws the captain's silver out, or cook the cat!'

Frankie began to load a tray with dishes for the mess deck. She counted the plates then stopped, brows raised.

'Taff, how could I? We've not got a cat!'

'Mebbe not. If we had I reckon you'd chuck it overboard, boyo! A dream, that's what you are. Often I seen you, staring into space with your mouth open, thousands of miles away.'

Frankie, mindful of Trevor's manners when he had been a mere sixteen-year-old, blew a raspberry.

'I dream in my own time, Taffy, and work in the firm's. That's my privilege.'

Taffy laughed, but did not dispute this piece of wisdom.

The *Arctic Glow* moved steadily northwards and as darkness fell, Frankie wearily picked up the slop bucket and prepared to take it up on deck. The men and the officers had eaten, she and Taff had eaten, and now that all was shipshape and Bristol fashion in the galley she only had to empty the slops before joining the rest of the crew on the mess deck, save for those currently on watch. Evenings were the best time, she reflected now as she mounted the companionway. In the evenings the captain never came on to the mess deck and the men were able to be themselves. Beer was handed out, cards were produced and tales told. She had only enjoyed two of these sessions, but enjoyed was definitely the word.

Curled up in a corner listening to the idle talk, the boasting, the crudeness and the sudden flashes of humour, she knew herself priveleged. She was sharing an exclusively male world in a way which would have been impossible had they known her secret.

On the deck the wind raked at the soft waves of golden-brown hair which tumbled across her forehead, making her shiver as she threw the rubbish over the rail—careful, of course, to do so to leeward. Walking back, she glanced quickly up at the bridge, but there was no sign of the captain. Jammy was standing by the radar and Dodger was at the helm. Frankie immediately felt a lifting of tension, knowing herself unobserved by those sharp grey eyes. She headed for the companionway, swinging her bucket, and almost put her foot on something dark and soft which moved and gave a horrid, strangling sqawk as her boot touched it.

'Ugh!' Frankie jumped back, heart thumping, then bent to look more closely at the object. 'What on earth...?'

A hand reached out of the darkness, nearly making her heart stop. It closed over the object.

'It's a pigeon,' The captain lifted the bird into the light from the bridge, displaying its smooth, smoke-grey plumage and a bright, white-ringed eye. 'A racing pigeon I expect.

They get blown off course and take refuge on any craft which is in their vicinity.' He held the bird out to Frankie. 'Take it to the galley.'

Frankie put her hands behind her back.

'What, to eat? Oh no, sir! Do let it go!'

He caught her arm and drew her into the companionway, closing the door on the wind. Then he unwound his muffler and stood looking down at her, his mouth rueful, the dark wing of hair falling across his forehead.

'What d'you think I am? No mariner would eat an exhausted bird, not even the ancient one! No, we feed them, then release them. This bird can't fly, don't you understand? He's exhausted.'

Frankie put out her hands and took the soft, warm bird. Beneath her fingers she could feel the tiny tapping of its heart.

'Sorry, Skipper, but when you said "take it to the galley" it sounded just like "take her to the tower". I'll look after it.'

'Very well. Do you know how? If not, Taff does.'

'I'll manage. Taff's on the mess deck.'

He glanced at his watch. She noticed that it was a heavy gold one and wondered idly where he had got such an expensive looking timepiece.

'I'll show you what to do.' Before she could protest that she was quite capable of dealing with the bird he had pushed her into the galley and followed her inside. 'Get a box, and some straw. The stuff the bottles come in will do.'

She found a box and some wood shavings and handed them to him. He had taken the bird from her, but now he placed it gently on the shavings and stood up.

'Now some saltines, I think, in a saucer. Float them in...' he was in Taff's beloved pantry and emerged abruptly, with a half bottle of rum in his hand. 'I guessed the old blighter would have something salted away. Pour it over some dried peas and put in some bits of bacon fat, and his crop will be stuffed by morning.'

She found a saucer and filled it with the nauseous mixture he had suggested, then poured the rum in. She looked up at him, her nose wrinkling, and he nodded.

'That'll do. Now write a note and pin it to the outside of the door so that someone doesn't walk in later and tread on the creature. We don't want any accidents.'

She obeyed, using an empty sugar bag and an old stub of pencil. He watched her as she wrote, then fixed it to the door for her. Finally, he raised a hand and left her, presumably to return to the officers' cabin.

Frankie made her way to the mess deck. It was warm, with cigarette smoke hazing the air and men sprawled on every chair. Frankie curled up on the long bench next to Jammy and prepared to watch the game of stud poker being played nearby. It was not a very serious game, with advice and suggestions being shouted by various bystanders, and presently she tugged Jammy's sleeve.

'Jammy? There's a racing pigeon in the galley.'

Jammy had been engrossed in a violently coloured paperback but he glanced up at her and grinned.

'That so? Company for you. Two little pigeons together.'

Raker, a deckhand of immense strength with arms which had earned him his nickname, reached out and grabbed Jammy's book.

'Stop readin', you ignorant blighter, Frankie's trying to make conversation! Anyway, why's the lad a pigeon? Eh?'

'Cos he's green as grass. Just you wait though, till we dock. I'm goin' to take him to Barney's.'

There was a howl of derision from the four card players. One of them, Chuffy, leaned forward and cuffed Jimmy on the side of the head, then turned to Frankie.

'So old Jammy's going to teach you a thing or two, eh? That's a laugh! One little tattoo Jammy's got, and we ain't seen it yet, neither.'

Thus challenged Jammy stood up, shed a multitude of jerseys, a grey denim working shirt and a vest, then turned his sturdy torso around like a model, to a chorus of shrieks and whistles. Just beneath his right shoulder blade was a blood-red heart. Beneath it, the words "I love Lucy" still had a faint pinkness around the blue lettering.

'See? I told you I wuz going to get a tattoo!' He turned to Raker, who was leaning back in his chair shuffling the pack with a suspicious expertness. 'I've not seen *your* tattoos, Rake!'

'Nor you won't boy,' Raker responded with a grin. 'Only my wimmin see my tattoos.'

There was a universal shout of laughter and Jammy grabbed his clothes and began to dress again.

'Well, anyway, you all thought I wouldn't do it, an' that's the proof that I'm not yeller!' He pulled the final jersey down over his head and reached for a can of beer. Opening it, he drank it standing up and swaying with the ship's motion. 'Is everyone else tattooed?'

The older deckhands just grinned, but one or two of the younger men displayed brawny arms blue with pictures.

'Yeah, thought so. Everyone but this 'ere pigeon.'

Frankie, seeing that some comment was expected of her, said curiously: 'Does it hurt?

42

I might get one done when we dock. Only I wouldn't put an old *girl's* name on my back, I think that's daft.'

'Why not?' Jammy bristled. 'I don't mind who knows about Lucy.'

'You don't mind now,' Frankie admitted. 'But what about in a year? Or ten?'

'What's it matter?' Chuffy had a round face, with beady eyes which saw more than most. 'Us two-day millionaires don't take off more'n our boots, mostly. And when we does, it's generally after dark.'

There was more laughter, and the bosun handed round another supply of beer cans. Frankie leaned over to Chuffy, who sat in the chair nearest her.

'Why did you call yourselves two-day millionaires?'

'That's what the gals call us. Haven't you heard? It's 'cos we come back from a trip an' spend a fortune, then it's back to the Arctic for another few weeks.' He leaned over her, to Jammy, who sat on the bench at her other side. 'Jam! Git my book, you're sitting on it.'

Jammy fished under the leather cushion and drew out a magazine, which he gave to Frankie to hand on to Chuffy. She glanced down at it, then quickly away. The cover page depicted a woman, nude, in an unromantic but frank pose.

'Look at you, colouring up,' Chuffy remarked conversationally as he took the magazine. 'Ain't you ever seen a naked woman before, Frankie?'

Frankie, staring to answer, choked and got the giggles. Fortunately, the men had not the remotest idea why she had laughed but grinned with her, thinking to themselves that a lad without so much as down on his cheek would naturally find the remark amusing.

'Awright, awright, I s'pose you haven't,' Chuffy said, opening the magazine and staring at the pictures. 'D'you want a beer, Frankie? If not, I'll have yours.'

'I don't like it much,' Frankie admitted. 'Is there anything else?'

A can of coke was found and handed over; evidently, there had been galley boys before her who preferred soft drinks. Taffy, now mending a disastrously torn jersey, glanced sideways at her. He had paid little heed to the conversation until now, having been reading his way solidly through a cookery book, but with the changeover to darning, he obviously felt like putting his spoke in.

'Don't let this lot talk you into getting tattooed, boyo, it's a mug's game. Thirty years I've been at sea, and not a tattoo on me. They talked Spud into it, and I reckon that's why he split. It do 'urt, you know, and where's the point? To brand yourself, like a stupid sheep!'

'Garn! He's probably tattooed all over, only

it don't show against the black,' Chuffy said, grinning at the cook. 'Test of courage it is, Taff.'

Secure in the knowledge that her return to shore would also be her return to anonymity so far as the crew were concerned, Frankie took a drink of coke and then turned to Taffy.

'Branded? Yes, that is what it amounts to, but I might have a little one done. Just to show I'm not afraid of the pain, of course.'

The bosun snorted, putting down his cards.

'Pain? You don't know what pain is, you young 'uns. Nowadays they do it all with electricity and in a minute. Clean, too, I daresay. When my Dad went to sea it was visiting some old feller in a backstreet week after week, for quite a simple design. And some of 'em went septic, too. You could lose an arm. Nasty.'

The card players suddenly gave a shout as Raker displayed his hand and scooped the pool towards him. He sat back in his chair, grinning at them all, their money in front of him.

'Like another game? No? What are you, men or mice? Well, pass me another beer, then.'

Jammy had abandoned his book and was Indian wrestling with Spick. He was scarlet-faced as the older man, without apparent effort, pushed his arm over until his hand lay flat on the mess table. Then he turned to Frankie.

'Come on, tiddler, I'll have a match with you. Best of three.'

'He's bent of beating someone, if only the tiddler,' Spick observed. 'Go on tiddler, show him up!'

'I don't believe you're sixteen,' Jammy remarked disgustedly as Frankie's hand met the table three times in quick succession. 'You've not got any muscle!'

Frankie grinned.

'You could be right.' She did not add that she was, in fact, eighteen. That really would be asking for groans of disbelief! 'What makes you say that, Jammy? Were you beating deckie learners when you were sixteen?'

'At your age he was galley boy aboard the *Boy Augustus,* and too busy being sick and stealing doughnuts to play at wrestling,' Chuffy said. He cocked his head to one side. 'Weather's blowing up. Who's on watch?'

'Pat and Wally,' the Bosun said. 'You on the next watch, Chuffy?'

'No, it's me night off. Pass us another can.'

It was at this point that Frankie, looking round her, realised that most of the men had already left for their bunks. The men who remained were those who had drunk a good deal of beer and she stood up, yawning, not wanting to remain here if the men descended to horseplay.

'I'm off to bed. Got an early start tomorrow.'

Chuffy reached out and grabbed her by the sleeve of her shaggy sweater.

'Not so fast, tiddler. Can you play dominoes?'

Spick and Jammy, yawning, were leaving the mess deck. Frankie shook her head.

'Afraid not, Chuff. Goodnight!'

She tried to tug herself free but Chuffy hung on, an obstinate expression on his flushed face.

'I'll teach you, then. Siddown!'

She had little choice but to obey as he jerked her on to the bench beside him. Frankie blinked nervously round the empty mess deck. She had no desire to play dominoes or anything else with Chuffy!

'Now. You ain't never been tattooed. That right?'

Frankie shifted uneasily on the leather cushion.

'That's right. What's that got to do with playing dominoes?'

He ignored the remark, continuing with his own train of thought.

'But you say you'll get done when we're back in port, just to prove you ain't scared of the pain. Right?'

47

'I said perhaps,' Frankie muttered. 'I only said...'

'You said you would,' Chuffy insisted. "Right. Well, I can tattoo. I'll do you one right now. What'd you like? A bleedin' heart? Two hearts, with an arrow through 'em? Eh?'

To her absolute horror, Frankie saw that Chuffy now held the great thick darning needle with which Taffy had been mending his sweater. She felt perspiration spring out on her forehead.

'Chuffy! You can't! You wouldn't!'

A glance at his face proved her wrong. The beer had brought a brightness to his eyes and sweat sheened his skin; the expression on his mouth frightened her. She tried to get up and he twisted her hands behind her back in a half nelson and jerked her to her feet. Before she could do more than yelp he had laid her, face down, on the mess table, her arms still bent up, her wrists held easily in one powerful hand.

His fingers fumbled at her clothing and she tried to twist away, only to feel her arms thrust further up her back, bringing a moment of pain so sickening that she groaned. Then air touched her bare back. Her heart was pounding so loudly that it seemed to shake the table.

'Here we are. Just remember, the pain only lasts a minute.'

48

She felt something rest lightly on her back, then press deeply into the skin beneath her right shoulder blade. She was rigid now, but with fear of discovery rather than fear of pain. If she moved carelessly she might pull the jersey further up her front, and then... She closed her eyes. Dear God, why couldn't help arrive?

She felt the needle again and could not prevent a tiny gasp. She felt blood trickle across her skin and Chuffy said cheerfully: 'Sorry, went a bit deep then.' Another jab, and fresh fear. Suppose she fainted and he rolled her over?

'Don't shake, Frankie, keep still!'

The admonition was unnecessary. Frankie would have given a lot to be able to stop shaking, but she did her best, drawing in her breath and holding it before gently expelling it on a long sigh.

The needle moved, jabbed, more blood trickled. And then the click of the door opening drove everything but the fear of discovery out of her head. She said, 'Please! Let me go!' and then, suddenly, her hands were free, her clothing hastily jerked down and she was struggling off the table.

Chuffy, red in the face, was confronting the intruder. It was the skipper.

'Just tattooing the tiddler, here, same's we did young Spud.' The captain's face might have been carved of ice and Chuffy, obviously unsure of his ground, cleared his throat uncertainly. 'You know, sir, only a laugh.'

'A laugh, Chuffy? Or bullying? Wally mentioned you'd been talking about tattooing and told me you'd scared the life out of young Spud. That's why I came down, to find out what mischief you were up to.'

'Sorry, sir. Only a joke, sir.' Abruptly, Chuffy grabbed Frankie, spun her round with her back to the captain, and tugged up her clothing again, to reveal his handiwork. 'See? No harm in it, sir.'

Frankie turned to face them again and saw, to her intense annoyance, that the captain was grinning, actually grinning!

'So I see. Very well, Chuffy, but no more of it, d'you understand?' He turned to Frankie. 'Off with you to your cabin.'

She shot past him, head lowered to hide the tears in her eyes. How could he dismiss it so lightly? She was sure that only a sadist could smile over her bloodstained back.

In her own cabin, she knelt and reached under the bunk for her soap and towel. She would go along and have a shower, and then at least she might keep the wounds free of infection. Now that she was away from the mess deck, reaction had set in and she was shaking like a leaf. The door opening behind her took her by surprise and she glanced over

50

her shoulder, eyes widening with fright. Suppose Chuffy had followed her in here to finish his handiwork?

But it was the skipper. He closed the door gently behind him, then walked towards her. His face was grim.

'You've seen the damage? I daresay it's all very light-hearted...' He stopped, seeing the whiteness of her face, the tearfilled eyes. 'You've not looked at your back yet?'

'No. But it bled, I felt it trickle when he pushed that dirty, rusty old needle into my s-skin.'

'Pull up your clothes.'

She put both arms round herself, hugging her jersey to her.

'No!'

In truth, she could scarcely have done so without revealing the upper half of her body to him as he stood there.

His mouth twitched.

'I see you can't. Hold on to the front, then.' He pulled up the back of her sweater, then moved her so that she could peer over her shoulder into the glass. 'See? You won't die of that!'

Written in wobbly biro letters between her shoulder blades was one word. SUCKER.

'But what about the blood?'

He peered closely at her back.

'Yes, something wet trickled down your

skin...' he rubbed her back, then laughed. 'The young sadist! Beer! He must have dripped some on to your skin to scare you more!'

'Oh! And I thought...' She gave a snort, a giggle, and then she began to sob; little, breath-catching sobs, such as a hurt child might give.

'Stop that! It's a joke, Frankie, not uncommon at sea. If you're going through with this you must take the rough with the smooth. If you're going to get hysterical I shall have to deal with you.'

She rubbed her eyes dry, and picked up her towel and the soap which had fallen to the floor when the captain touched her.

'Sorry. I was afraid I'd faint, and he might...might...'

'From fear, do you mean?' Was there contempt in the light grey eyes? 'You mustn't faint, must you?'

The menace in his tone was unmistakable. Dumbly, she shook her head.

'Then clean yourself up, get to bed, and forget it.' He crossed to the door, put his hand out to open it, and paused. 'Another thing, don't ever let yourself be manoeuvred into being alone with one of the men again.'

'I'm alone with you.'

He turned, a sardonic smile on his lips.

'Ah, but I'm different! After all, if you are discovered, you'll find yourself condemned to my company day and night! If you don't want that to happen, don't tempt fate. Goodnight.'

He opened the door and strode out of the cabin and down the corridor towards his own quarters. Frankie, towel and soap in her hands, stared after him for a moment, then headed for the showers. Should she be grateful to him for rescuing her? But Chuffy had only been trying to make a fool of her! On the other hand, if the captain had not interrupted, suppose Chuffy, with no thought other than to enjoy the joke to the full, had decided to write something rude across her chest?

She winced at the thought and decided that she was grateful to the captain. She also thought that it was her duty to make sure nobody tried any similar practical jokes on her. Standing beneath the shower, the warm water cascading down and washing off the lather, Frankie mused on a suitable revenge.

3

Rather to Frankie's surprise, the tattooing episode had raised her stock considerably amongst the deckhands.

'Not a whimper nor yet a wail,' Chuffy had apparently reported to his mates. 'He was pale, mind, but he hopped off the table bold as brass and went to 'is cabin and then to the showers to scrub up.'

Although no one remarked on it, Frankie also had her suspicions that he had not much relished his cascara-laden coffee, unsuspectingly drunk next morning. She had done her best to see that everyone knew she was responsible for his discomfiture and therefore not to be trifled with, by drawing wide-eyed attention to his frequent absences next day.

But for whatever cause, the men now regarded her as one of themselves. Invitations to show her how to mend a net, to explain how the trawl was shot, to teach her stud poker, were extended and accepted. The crew were a man short too, so she was pressed into service in a thousand small ways and her willingness, the good natured way in which she undertook such tasks, endeared her to men well used to lazy young good-for-nothings in the galley, who never raised a finger unless bawled out by the cook.

To be sure, there had been trouble over the pigeon, but even that, it seemed, was forgiven her.

As the captain had ordered, she had carried the pigeon up on deck at seven o'clock the next day, and put it down on the hatch cover. The bird squatted there, fuffling its feathers irritably in the wind, cooing anxiously, fixing her with its beady eye. After a few seconds, it hopped down and scuttled for shelter by Frankie's feet, rubbing against her for all the world like a fat, domesticated cat.

She tried to get rid of the bird conscientiously for ten minutes, then picked it up and took it back to the galley. To Taffy's warning that the Skipper would not be pleased, she shrugged. How would he ever find out, she demanded. Who would tell him? And how likely was it that the captain of the ship would go prowling around the galley and find out for himself?

Which only proved how little she knew, she thought afterwards. Because the captain had to pass the galley a dozen or more times each day, so the notice had to come down off the door. And, inevitably, someone left the door open and her feathered friend had got out.

Where had it chosen to roost? Upon whose books had it left innumerable little reminders of its presence? Who had returned to his cabin, late at night, tired out, to find filthy footmarks on his sheets, filthy feathers on his carpet, and a filthy pigeon doing filthy things on his bookshelves? Who else but the one person on board who had not known of the bird's presence? The skipper, naturally!

His roar had brought Frankie, quivering, out of her bunk, to rescue her pet and then to return to his cabin with brush and dustpan, a bowl of disinfected water and a cloth. As she had brushed and cleaned he had given his opinion freely of her brain power— none—, her commonsense—nil—, and her deceitfulness—considerable. It had been the most comprehensive telling-off that she had ever received in a life studded with them.

But though he warned her, through gritted teeth, that it would have served her and her wretched bird right if he had hurled it off the ship himself, he also told her that it was now too late. The bird would never live in the arctic conditions already prevailing on deck. It would be allowed to stay.

Frankie's fervent thanks had only annoyed him more, it seemed.

'I'm not letting the creature stay to reward you,' he told her repressively. 'So don't look so pleased with yourself. I'm letting it stay because the men are superstitious. Now put that notice back on the door and clear out!'

She had gone, happy in the knowledge that the pigeon would be allowed to remain on board now, probably until they decked at Grimsby once more.

So now she stood in the galley, waiting for Taffy to pour the drinks for the bridge, very content with her lot. Jammy, bursting through the door, brought her head round, brows arching.

'What is it?'

'Land! Come up and see, Frankie!'

Taffy nodded to her, so she hastily put on her coat and muffler and followed Jammy up on deck.

It was very cold and dusk seemed to have fallen, though it was scarcely that late in the day. The sea heaved tumultuously and through the clear-view window onto the bridge she could see the mate and the skipper moving about. She hoped they were not looking out, wondering what mischief she was up to this time.

'Look! Over there, through the mist...that's Bear Island.'

She followed the direction of Jammy's finger and saw, black and grim, the great shoulders of the island humping out of the fog.

'Gosh. Does anyone live there?'

Jammy shook his head.

'Not the way you mean, anyway. There's a harbour, and I think people are there in the summer. But not living, just staying a bit.'

'I see.' The two of them reached the rail and Frankie looked over, into the emerald swell.

'Why's the sea so green, Jammy?'

The two had to shout above the wind and since Jammy merely shrugged and caught at her arm, she suspended her questions until they were in the shelter of the companion-way. And then Jammy got his question out first.

'Well? What d'you think of the Arctic, tiddler? Not much like Southend, eh?'

'Exciting! Though it's a bit dark.'

Jammy grinned and pushed her ahead of him, down the corridor and into the galley.

'It'll be darker soon. It's eternal night where we're going. And don't look so excited, kiddo, because it's nothing to us but freezing cold, danger and if we're lucky, fish!'

As they entered the room Taffy turned, the kettle in his hand.

'Get a jug and mugs pronto, Frankie, the bridge want their coffee.'

'What about me?' Jammy queried plaintively. 'It's brass monkey weather out there, Taff, honest.'

'Righto, Jammy, get a mug then!'

58

Frankie had filled her jug and now she was sorting through a tin of biscuits, finding a good selection which she put into her pocket. Jammy, both hands round his coffee mug, sidled over to the biscuit tin.

'Ooh, biscuits! Give us one, tiddler.'

Frankie sorted out a few plain biscuits and pushed them across the table.

'Don't say I never give you anything. Get out of the light now, Jammy, I don't want to tip coffee everywhere.'

She made her way to the bridge to find the captain conning the ship while Wally, the mate, stood at the helm. She handed the Mate a mug, then filled it for him and fished out some biscuits, which she slipped into his pocket. Then she went over to the captain. He was bent over the radar but took the mug she offered automatically, holding it steady whilst she poured though he continued to stare into the screen. He took a mouthful of coffee, then caught her shoulders, manoeuvring her in front of him so that she could see the screen.

'See those dots?'

The radar was a mystery to her. She could see the amber screen with the beam of light ceaselessly turning, illuminating as it went large dots, small dots, and a ragged sort of outline which scattered as the beam touched it a tiny comet-tail of fizzing sprays and specks of light. But it meant nothing to her. However, she examined it closely, screwing her eyes up the better to concentrate.

'Yes, I see them. What do they mean?'

He indicated the dots with the tip of a pencil.

'These are ships, mostly. And these...' moving the pencil to more dots, '...are rocks. This bit...' running the pencil above the ragged outline, '...is Bear Island—a land mass always looks like that.'

'I see. It's a picture of what's ahead and around.'

He was bent over her, his hands resting lightly on her shoulders and the fingers moved almost imperceptibly, as if he was gently massaging her small bones through the thicknesses of her jerseys. A frisson of feeling—was it fear?—tingled along her backbone and she shifted uneasily.

'Is that all, Skipper?'

He said nothing, merely moving her along to where another instrument stood. Here a pencil traced continually on a piece of paper a line, sometimes straight, sometimes wobbly. She stared at it, too aware of the captain's proximity to be able to give it all her attention. His breath was actually stirring the hair above her left ear and his chest was touching her shoulder blades.

'This is the Echo Sounder. The pencil draws

the bottom for us so that we see when we're over rocks, or wrecks, undersea mountains, valleys.'

'I see. Are there many wrecks here?'

'More than in any other part of the ocean, I believe. The biggest and bloodiest naval battle of the last war was fought in these waters. Even now, nearly forty years afterwards, the fleet trawl up mines, great rusty ship's plates, equipment. It's a haunted place. We never trawl here.'

'Good,' Frankie said fervently. She stood back, watching him as he drained his coffee mug. She took it from him, then turned to take the mate's. He had finished the coffee but was munching a biscuit which made Frankie's hand fly to the pocket. She had not given the skipper his share.

She turned back, to where he stood by the radar.

'Sir...I'm sorry. I didn't give you your biscuits.'

He did not look up.

'That's all right. Shove them into my pocket.'

The mate was wearing a jacket, but the captain was not. She stared at him, nonplussed. He had no pockets in that big shelland sweater. Did he mean the pockets in his dark trousers? She swallowed. It seemed a bit...

Quickly, before she could change her mind or lose her nerve, she crammed the biscuits into his trouser pocket, her face turned away, feeling acutely self-conscious. Then, before she could be asked to do anything else, she hurried off the bridge and back to familiar warmth and safety of the galley.

'I've taken the bridge their coffee,' she said breathlessly, going over to the sink to rinse the mugs. 'Where's Dolly Parton?'

The pigeon had been nicknamed Dolly Parton for obvious reasons, and all Frankie's efforts to make the men call it something different failed dismally. Dolly Parton it would remain. Taffy, rolling out what appeared to be several yards of his light and delicious pastry, pointed beneath the kitchen table with his rolling pin.

'On my feet. More like a broody 'en than a racing pigeon she is. Sparks read the leg-number over the radio and seems she's from my part of the country. Supposed to be flying from Norway to Cardiff she was, blown a bit off course, like.'

'Poor Doll! But we'll take her back as far as Grimsby, won't we, Taff?'

'Aye, no reason why not. Might even cadge a lift for her if we meet a trawler bound for Fleetwood or somewhere up that way. Only we must be careful she don't get out, see? Put one of them little pink feet on the deck from now on, and it's curtains for Dolly.'

'Is that so?' Frankie could not help sounding sceptical. 'What about the gulls, then? They do all right.'

'You don't know the half, son. Dolly Parton ain't built to withstand Arctic conditions any more than we are. And when we get further north you'll see gulls drop on to the deck frozen stiff.'

'Oh, sure! Covered with tattoos, I suppose?'

Taffy reached for a bag of currants and began to sprinkle the dried fruit generously over his pastry. He cast her a reproachful look as he did so.

'Did I have any hand in that business? Well, did I? I wouldn't make a fool of me own galley boy. You'll see, that's what!'

'I'm sorry, Taffy, I shouldn't scoff. I do believe you really. What shall I do next? The vegetables?'

Together the two of them worked through the day. Frankie took hot drinks to the bridge, and the last time found that Raker and Matthew, a man obviously destined for promotion, were on watch.

'Skipper's taking over later, so we'll probably shoot the trawl at about midnight,' Raker guessed, taking his hot drink carefully in one hand. 'Got any butties?'

Frankie nodded and offered one of the somewhat squashed cheese sandwiches, wedged in between the coffee jug and her sweater.

'Yes, but it's the last of the bread. Taff's making some more tomorrow though, or rather he's going to reach me to make it.'

Matthew leaned over and helped himself to the remaining cheese sandwich.

'Thanks for the warning, sunshine; I'll eat well today and starve tomorrow. Here, hang onto the wheel for a minute.'

Frankie grabbed for the wheel and left, for the first time, the surge and buck of the ship as she met the waves. She hung on with both hands, thankful that Matthew's sinewy fingers were still grasping the wheel or it would have spun helplessly.

'Why does it fight to get free?' she demanded rather aggrievedly when Matthew had finished his sandwich and reclaimed the helm. 'You all make it look so easy!'

'Rotation of the earth. Ask the skipper, he'll explain,' Matthew said. 'Arctic waters are the most dangerous in the world, Frankie, because of currents, and the fearful winds which never stop, so the sea's always rough. How's Dolly Parton?'

Giving a progress report, Frankie reflected on the strangeness of the male race, and of trawlermen in particular. They seemed a coarse, rough crowd with their pornographic magazines, their crude jokes and their talk larded with swear-words. Yet each man on board was as concerned over the pigeon's fate as she herself was, and each would willingly spend time and effort on any sick bird which landed on their small but indomitable craft.

That evening, Frankie served the officers with stew and dumplings followed by currant duff and custard, and noticed that the captain was unusually abstracted, scarcely speaking whilst she was in the cabin. She mentioned this fact to Taffy when she returned to the galley and was duly enlightened.

'He's doing the night-trick,' Taffy explained. 'Everyone thinks we'll shoot the trawl tonight, but the skipper's the only one who knows for sure. You get some rest now, then come to the galley for 10.30 and you can take him a mug of tea to start his watch.

'All right. Do I take it to his cabin or to the bridge.'

'To his cabin. He'll be there now, snatching a few hours sleep before his watch.'

Frankie spent the early evening playing cards on the mess deck and at ten fifteen, went along to the galley. Taffy explained that it was a courtesy to wake the captain, but that even when they were trawling, the men usually came down to the galley for any hot drinks and food they wanted so that the cook and his boy could have a good night's sleep.

She put the kettle on and when it boiled, made the tea and carried a mug along to the captain's cabin. She tapped on the door, scarcely expecting an answer, then opened it and went in.

The skipper lay on his back, his face relaxed in sleep. Frankie stole over to the bed and looked down at him. He looked much younger, dark, stubby lashes closed, hair rumpled, mouth gentled.

'Skipper? Wake up, sir!' She nudged him gently with her knee, holding the mug steady. 'Tea's here, Skipper.'

As she watched, he woke and the illusion of gentleness vanished. His grey eyes focussed sharply on her face, then he propped himself up on one elbow and held out his hand, half-smiling at her. Immediately, in a reflex action, she stepped back. Tea, scalding hot, splashed onto his outstretched hand. The smile vanished.

'Damn it, what the devil are you playing at?'

'Sorry, Skipper, it was...the movement of the ship.'

She thrust the mug into his hand and turned to make for the door.

'Wait!'

She turned, reluctantly, to see him swinging his legs out of his bunk. He was wearing his trousers and nothing else.

'Yes, sir?'

'Pass me my clothes and wait for the mug.'

She had forgotten in her panic the unwritten rule: one did not hand a mug of hot drink to a busy man on board ship, for should he need to stand the mug down for a moment, where could he do so? Nowhere was safe. She reached for his clothes, a great many of them, for all the men wore a number of garments, knowing that the warm air trapped between each layer would keep them from freezing better than one thick garment would have done.

'Here they are. Sorry, sir.'

He drank half the hot tea, then handed her the mug and picked up a t-shirt. She watched idly as he pulled it on, then reached for a conventional shirt. He put it on, buttoned it, and then proceeded to undo his trousers in order to push the shirt in around the waistband.

Quickly, she averted her eyes, but not before she had seen him give her a quizzical glance. She blushed, looking fixedly away, hearing him pull the zip up again, knowing he was pulling one of his thick-knit, fisherman's jerseys on over his head. He chuckled, then whisked the tea out of her hand and

67

drained the mug, catching her shoulder as he finished and turning her round to face him.

'You're a galley-boy! Remember our bargain? Just forget...' his hand stole round the back of her neck, the fingers pushing into the soft hair which curled at the nape. '...forget girlish scruples. You're a man amongst men, and I must behave as I always do. I'm due on the bridge, you need my mug. See?'

She looked up at him, an apology trembling on her lips—and said not a word. He was looking at her almost gently, with a kind of rueful understanding, swaying easily on the balls of his feet, telling her to be a man amongst men...and when he looked like that, touched her hair...Without a word she grabbed his empty mug and made for the door. 'I know, sir. Sorry, sir.'

She was through the doorway and in the corridor, her heart going overtime, panting as if she had run a race. Whatever is the matter with me? She wondered, going slowly along to the galley. He is, without doubt, a bully and an arrogant man. Then how is it, when he touches me, that my knees turn to water and I have to fight an impulse to throw myself on his chest and beg him to take care of me? She flinched at what his probable answer would be to such an appeal. She must be mad!

Back in the galley, with Dolly gurgling

away to herself from her box near the stove, she rinsed the mug and returned it to its hook. Then she checked that everything was in its place before going out into the corridor again, closing the door carefully behind her. She would get some sleep now, and perhaps she might wake when they shot the trawl so that she could see for herself what happened.

Someone banging against her door as they passed brought her eyes wide open. It was dark but she could see a line of light under her door and the ship's crew were very much awake. Boots thundered on the decking, voices called. She lay for a moment wondering whether to get up or not, but curiosity got her out of bed. She struggled into her clothes and made her way out into the corridor. Jammy came out of his cabin at a run, grinning as he pushed past her.

'You up, tiddler? They've just hauled the log and we're shooting the trawl any moment. Get a coat on and come and watch!' Frankie stumbled in the galley, wrapped up warmly, and made her way up the companionway and onto the deck. It was pitch dark and bitterly cold, the arc-lights which lit the deck showed the sea to be so rough that occasionally a wave would crash down right across the deck, soaking everyone. The deckhands were all in oilskins and moving purposefully across the tilting, slippery deck. She glanced up at the bridge. Wally, the mate, was standing near the open bridge window and the captain stood the other side of it, with Sparks at the helm. Even as she watched, the captain cast one keen glance at the sea and the trawl, lashed to the deck, then leaned well out, taking the wind full in the face so that his hair blew up in a plume.

'Cod End outboard! Let go!'

The trawl shot down into the sea and Frankie, clinging to the edge of the companionway, heard the telegraph on the bridge ring for Slow Ahead. Craning her neck, she could see the pale floats surging on the swell, then the ship shuddered as some other part of the trawl crashed down. She glanced up at the bridge, to see the Captain gesturing frantically at her. Faint against the noise of the wind she heard his words.

'Back! Get back!'

She saw another big sea coming and hastily climbed back inside the companionway, slamming the door behind her. The water rattled against it and, conscience-stricken, she tried to hurry past the bridge door. But he was waiting for her. He wasted no time in reproaches however, but his hard hands grabbed her and hauled her unceremoniously into the bridge, then spun her round and ran her over to stand by the wheel.

It was cold and noisy in the bridge, because of the open window. Pinned beside the wheel with her nose practically pressed against the glass, Frankie started to speak to the captain, and was peremptorily silenced.

'Shut up and watch!'

She glanced at his face and obeyed. It was almost cruel with concentration, the bleak eyes steady on the men, the mouth held so tight that a line was drawn between lips and nostril. He flicked a glance at her when he saw the triangle of her face turn towards him and for a moment she read cold contempt in his eyes. Then he turned his gaze back to the deck and she knew herself forgotten, or at least totally disregarded.

For a moment she was chilled. She had been a fool to stand on the deck, but she had not known! But presently, the sheer fascination of watching men supremely competent at their job took over. She stayed where she was because she wanted to stay, because nothing short of physical violence would have dragged her away from her lookout.

She watched the warp paid out and fathom marks glide over the side. The winchmen applied the brakes to the winch and the ship appeared to come to a dead halt, rearing up like a horse when a strong man heaves on the reins. The skipper leaned out of his window once more, braced against the wind.

'Hook on!' He roared, his hands making light work of what Frankie guessed must in reality be a fighting wheel. He leaned sideways to peer at his instruments, then back to watch the trawl with unswerving intentness. He flicked a quick glance at the echo sounder again, then leaned through the window.

'Let her go!'

As he spoke, he put the wheel over hard and the ship heeled, making Frankie gasp. But it had been expected on the deck, not a man moved. The Bosun, watching the trawl, turned and shouted up to the bridge.

'She's all square, Boss, and level aft!'

The skipper indicated that he had heard, then slammed the window shut. He reached for the telegraph and returned it to ring for Half Ahead, and beneath her feet the engines, which had stopped whilst the trawl was shot, roared into life once more.

Below the bridge window, the men were strolling back to the quarterdeck and disappearing into the companionway. She glanced at her watch. The whole operation had barely taken eight minutes!

She turned back into the bridge. Relaxation and relief were almost tangible things. The Sparks turned away from his watch on the radar and grinned affably at Frankie.

'What did you think of that, tiddler?'

'It was great! They're a great team, aren't they! What happens next?'

The skipper took her shoulder and pushed her towards the bridge door.

'Bed. For three hours. Then we haul.' They left the room together and strolled down the corridor towards their berths. 'Want waking then?'

'Yes, please. I'd hate to miss it.'

'Right. And don't think I've forgotten your behaviour earlier. Don't *ever* go on deck again when we're shooting or hauling, unless you want to be killed.'

He did not wait for a reply but turned into his cabin and Frankie continued on to her own berth. She was exhilarated and awed by what she had seen and knew she would be unlikely to sleep with the knowledge that she had a mere three hours to wait before the next act in the drama was played out. She lay down on her bunk however, fully clothed but for boots and coat and wondered, for the first time, whether he had been warning her that she could easily be killed out on deck when trawling was going on, or whether he meant that he would kill her with his own hands if she ever behaved in such an irresponsible manner again.

Puzzling over it, she could only conclude that either was equally possible!

4

It seemed as though she had barely closed her eyes before her door shot open with a clatter and a hand switched the light on. She pushed her face into the pillow, and felt a hand on her shoulder, shaking her awake.

'Up! Bring coffee!'

She opened her eyes in time to see the Captain disappearing round her cabin door. For a moment she wondered what was happening, where she was, then she remembered and shot upright like a jack-in-the-box. They were hauling! She was out of bed instantly, cramming on her boots and coat, winding the muffler round her face and then hesitating. The Captain had said something about taking a drink to the bridge, hadn't he? She seemed to remember the word coffee, or had she dreamed it? She decided it must have been part of her dream and tucked the ends of the muffler into her coat. She did not intend to waste her time making coffee when at any moment the catch would be revealed. If they want coffee they can wait for it, she thought grimly, trotting along toward the bridge.

She entered the room and the skipper glanced around from the radar screen.

'Coffee?'

She opened her mouth to say she would fetch it later, that she was desperate to watch every moment of the haul — and shut it without a word. She found herself in the galley, putting the kettle on, scarcely knowing how she had got there. Dolly opened one ringed eye, blinked, then closed it firmly. She was perching on a piece of broom handle which Taffy had propped across the box, and obviously felt that night was for sleeping in, and no one should disturb her!

Wide awake by now, Frankie made the coffee, put the lid on the jug and picked up two mugs. Then she made her way back to the bridge. This time, her reception was a little more brusque, if anything.

'Here!'

She obeyed instantly, standing between the skipper, who had the window wide open and one hand on the wheel, and the sparks, watching the instruments. Then she handed the sparks a mug, filled it and with a glance at the skipper, filled the other mug. As soon as he moved away from the activities on the deck outside she handed him the mug.

'Coffee, sir.'

'Thanks.' He drank, then handed her back

the mug and wiped his mouth with the back of his hand. 'Is she steady, Len?"

The sparks had the wheel now and he nodded. At once, the skipper leaned out of the window.

'Let go!'

The men had been standing easily in what was obviously a well-rehearsed pattern, each man ready to jump to his appointed task. With the skipper's bellowed order they swung into action. Someone swung a hammer, the winchmen raced to their winch, other deckhands rushed to guidelines. The skipper rang for half speed and then, almost at once, for stop. The sparks hauled the wheel over and the winch drums gathered speed; the trawl appeared above the surface.

For the next few moments she could not follow the movements, exclamations, orders. The bag, known as the Cod End, came clear of the sea and was swung over the deck, then lowered. The mate stepped up to it, heaved on a rope, the net opened and a silvery flood of fish crashed on to the deck. A silvery flood, yet it barely covered the floor of the pound. Frankie heard the skipper exclaim beneath his breath, a bitter, one word curse, then he picked up his empty mug from the floor and held it out to her. She filled it and watched him drink. He slammed the mug back into her waiting hand without a word or a glance, then leaned out of the window again.

'All clear out there?'

Frankie heard the bosun's roar of 'Aye aye,' and then the skipper was shouting again.

'Cod End outboard! Let her go!'

She watched, astonished, as the whole procedure was reversed and the trawl returned to the sea. When they were towing once again and the deckhands had trooped back below, she dared a remark.

'You put the trawl back at once, then?'

He nodded, frowning over the chart.

'Yes. We're here to catch fish.'

Frankie shuffled her feet.

'Yessir. That wasn't a good catch though, was it?'

'No.' He turned to the sparks, at the helm. 'We'll haul in three hours of course, but the men had best eat before then. Who's on watch?'

Sparks considered.

'It must be Tom and Spick, Skipper.'

He nodded, then turned back to Frankie.

'Have the watch call you at six forty, then the men can eat at seven.'

'Aye aye, sir.'

She left the bridge, suddenly aware of how tired she was. She wondered where she would find the men about to go on watch, and was contemplating a visit to the mess deck when suddenly, the door of the galley shot open and Spick came out with several cans of beer clasped lovingly in his arms and two of the ungainliest sandwiches she had ever seen balanced on top of them. He hailed her with relief.

'Here, tiddler, catch hold of these.'

Frankie took the sandwiches and smiled at Spick's anxiously furrowed brow.

'Why should I? I'm going to bed!'

'No you aren't, matey, or not till you've carried my butties to the bridge for me!'

Without more ado he set off for the bridge with Frankie, grasping the sandwiches, close behind. Once there, he put the cans of beer down in the swivel chair in front of the radio and took the sandwiches from her hands. The captain and the sparks had already gone to their berths but the bosun was coping quite well alone, it seemed, though he turned around and rubbed his hands at the sight of the beer in his colleague's arms.

'Good for you, Spick. Off with you, Frankie, you look worn out.'

'I am tired,' Frankie admitted. 'But the skipper wants breakfast at seven, so could one of you wake me at six forty, please? And Taff?'

'We'll do that,' the Bosun said. 'When shall we get the hands up?'

Frankie shrugged halfway out of the bridge door already, eager for her bed.

'If breakfast's at seven, about ten to the hour will do, I should think. Thanks.'

They trawled without much success for fifteen hours, then the captain had the trawl lashed and announced that they would steam north. The *Arctic Glow* butted her way through increasingly rough seas, with the weather worsening all the time. There were grumbles over the course being steered—Raker, an old hand at arctic fishing remarked grimly that uncharted waters the best fishing could also bring disaster.

They were in perpetual polar darkness now, with only their lights to illuminate the deck and a small area of the surrounding sea but the work and life of the ship went on as before, with Frankie serving the men on watch and helping Taffy cook extra delicious meals. They did everything they could in this way to compensate for the wicked cold and the hard work which would presently begin again.

Frankie had seen her first iceberg, watching with awe as the searchlight caught the great mountain of ice, striking diamonds, sapphires and emeralds off every facet as they turned to avoid her. To Frankie, the iceberg was female, a beautiful, jewelled witch riding on the seaswell, with a female's allure in her sparkling depths—and death for them all if the ship got too close and struck the great mass of submerged ice by which she was surrounded.

Now, standing in the steaming galley where Taffy was boiling a suet pudding of immense proportions, on the stove-top, she thought she heard a difference in the engine note. After a moment she asked Taffy if they had slowed down. Taffy was peeling potatoes at the sink but he stopped for a moment, cocking his head to listen.

'You're right. Tell you what, boyo, take the slop bucket up and ask one of the deckies, or whoever's on watch. Someone'll know. They always do.'

Wrapped up, with her mittened hands clutching the slop bucket, Frankie ventured forth. She was used to the cold, but when she put her nose outside the door she knew at once that this was different. Ice coated the deck, the rails, the masts and rigging. In the arc-lights it looked beautiful, but totally unreal. If one had seen a stage set like this, Frankie thought, one would have praised the artist's imagination, never dreaming that it had been copied from reality. She glanced around her. No one else was on deck, though figures moved about on the bridge. Then, suddenly, the arc-lights were doused. She sighed to herself. That meant they wouldn't be trawling yet.

Crossing the deck was not easy even with her sturdy boots but she reached the rail and stood the bucket down for a moment. Then a strange phenomenon caught her eyes and she leaned over the rail, looking down into the black, surging sea beneath them. It was neither snowing nor hailing, yet there seemed to be particles of black ice actually rising out of the sea, like a haze or fog. Whatever was it?

She watched for a moment longer, then reminded herself that she had work to do. She went to pick up her bucket, and realised she could not move. Her duffle coat and mittens were securely frozen to the ice-covered rail. Frankie gave a snort of amusement and tried to move back to give herself more purchase to tug her arms free. She stopped smiling. Her boots were frozen to the deck! This was frightening! She tried to shout, but her cry was no louder than a seagull's mew against the scream of the wind. She tried again, knowing that no one would hear her. Where, oh where, was someone?

She turned her head with difficulty and a fold of her muffler, frozen by her breath, scored against her cheek, bringing tears of pain to her eyes. The tears turned to ice on her cheeks. She called again, wrenching against the restricting clothing, but she was frozen far too firmly to the rail for any jerking of her own to help her. What could she do? She called again, then gave up. She was so terribly tired, she would just rest against the rail for a moment, close her eyes and rest; then perhaps she would have strength enough to...

She did not know how long she remained there, frozen into place like a dead sparrow. Dimly, from far away, she heard footsteps thumping across the deck behind her, felt arms tighten around her, knew she was being hacked and heaved free. She knew it was the skipper even in her semi-conscious state, she heard him swear, briefly, when he could not get her boots free. Then he simply lifted her out of them, leaving them frozen in place, and ran with her across the deck and down the companionway.

At first she could not feel the warmth, then the tears on her face melted and her cheeks and nose began to ache. She was crying, turning her face into the skipper's duffle coat, feebly trying to hide her weeping. He rushed her along the corridor and into the shower, propping her up in one corner like a frozen plank of wood whilst he shot the bolt across and turned the water to hot. Then, before she could protest, he was stripping off the heavy, iced duffle coat, the layers of sweaters, her jeans and socks and pants and pushing her, mother-naked, under the hot water.

She swayed and would have fallen and with an exclamation of impatience he held her up, drooping, whilst the water beat hot on her skin and she struggled to regain complete consciousness.

Then, suddenly, feeling began to return. The pain was intense and she cried out, her body flushed and steaming, the circulation of blood causing her to gasp, drawing the damp air into her lungs instead of taking shallow breaths. But now she was fighting to escape the jets of water, tears mingling with the water on her cheeks. How she ached! How the water stung!

'Get back under that shower, you stupid little bitch!' he gritted the words out through clenched teeth. 'Do you want to live?'

She scarcely heard, pain and shock mingling to make her mulishly determined to escape from the stinging water jets. She fell to her knees and began to crawl out and he jerked her upright, holding her shoulders, keeping her forcibly beneath the spray, his mouth in a tight, exasperated line.

'This if for your own good!'

He shook her, and she came round properly at last, knowing where she was and why. Simultaneously came realisation of her nakedness, the tiny cubicle in which they were enclosed, the locked door. Her eyes widened and flew to his and she saw, in the same instant, that he had scarcely thought about her nakedness either, in his haste to get the frost thawed out of her. But her own awareness had brought his about.

He was in his usual bridge gear, the white, roll-necked sweater and dark trousers tucked into sea-boots. Now, the sleeves of the sweater were pushed up to his elbows, the shower had sleeked his hair to his head with the spray which had bounced off the walls. Eyes narrowed against the spray gazed into hers, and she saw something flare in their depths. His hands slid down her arms and the backs of his fingers touched the flanks of breasts rosy from the heat, beaded with water. His eyes left her own, caressed her hardening nipples, her flat young belly; roved lower.

Frankie cringed back into the water, no longer wanting to escape from it. A frail curtain, it offered her suddenly an illusion of safety, some measure of protection from those suddenly intent grey eyes.

It was only an illusion. He moved towards her, pulling her at the same time into his arms and held her, wet and slippery as a fish, against him. His hands slithered with arrogant possessiveness across the skin of her back and hips and then, as she tried to pull away, he lowered his head and found her mouth.

She was back under the shower, the water was pattering on to her upturned face, forcing her to close her eyes. Then his head moved and she was sheltered. He gave an odd little noise in the back of his throat and she felt the blood tingle through her, felt, deep in her stomach, a surge of desire for him which he brought to a peak as his tongue deliberately probed her mouth and he slid one hand round to her breast, touching the nipple in such a way that the breath caught in her throat and she began to tremble, no longer wanting him to stop, caught in a web of emotions which were beyond understanding and could only be experienced.

He felt the trembling which racked her, and pushed her away so suddenly that she almost fell. He turned the water off, then reached for a large towel which hung behind the door.

'Rub yourself dry with this.'

For a moment she just stared, a sleeper awoken. Then shame that he had been the one to come to his senses, break the embrace, brought the colour flooding to her face. She wrapped the towel tightly round her nakedness and looked across at him through the steam which filled the cubicle.

85

He was soaked. Hair, sweater, trousers, boots. In that mad moment he must have stepped right into the shower with her, never thinking or caring about his clothing.

A little giggle burst out before Frankie could prevent it, but he looked so angry that she hastily turned away, beginning to rub herself with the towel. Standing on the raised tiles, he wrenched off his sweater and the t-shirt beneath it and began to kick off his boots. Strangely enough, this aroused very real terror in Frankie's bosom. Two minutes earlier she would have let him seduce her without a struggle, but now, watching him take his clothes off, she feared rape. She sidled round, trying to get near the door to unbolt it so that she could escape, careless of the fact that, wrapped so tightly in the towel, it would be only too obvious to anyone she might meet that she was no boy!

'Where do you think you're going?'

The words, barked out so sharply, insensibly, reassured her. Instinctively, she knew that had he meant to take her by force he would not have shouted in that manner!

'I thought if you were going to shower I'd go to my cabin.'

He laughed shortly.

'Don't worry, I've been in quite enough hot water for one night!' He leaned against the door, making it clear that she could not escape, his grey eyes uncomfortably knowing, uncomfortably mocking. 'Afraid?'

'Not any more. But cold.'

Immediately, the situation changed. He caught the towel and began vigorously rubbing her body all over until she was glowing, then he draped the towel decorously, so that her arms, beneath it, hid the swell of her small breasts.

'Bed, now,' he said, unbolting the door and ushering her out ahead of him. 'I'll see to our wet things. And I hope you've learned your lesson. Never stand still on deck, or touch anything. Not when there's black frost about.'

They reached her cabin without meeting anyone and he stepped inside, glancing critically around him.

'Hmm. Not exactly a home from home! Where's your spare clothing? Under the bunk? In the box?'

She nodded miserably, shivering in good earnest now.

He reached under the bunk and pulled out the box with Spud's warm clothing in it, and selected a pair of corduroys, two sweaters and a pair of thick socks. He held the first sweater out and she saw his eyes gleam as she primly held up the towel and somehow managed to scramble into the garment without revealing her breasts. He pulled the warm woollens down to her waist with apparent emotion, though when his fingers grazed the bare skin across her midriff she saw, in the back of his eyes, an echo of the feeling which had darkened his glance when he had taken her into his arms, in the shower.

'Put the socks on next. That's right. I'll leave you to put your trousers on without my help. Then get into bed.'

He left the cabin without more ado, and as soon as she had forced her trembling legs into the baggy corduroy trousers, she snuggled down in bed, pulling the grey blankets up round her ears, and the pain of aching flesh returned to make her moan, even as shock brought the shivering fit back.

He was back five minutes later with two hot water bottles and a mug of steaming cocoa. He made her sit up and fed her cocoa laced with rum, and he put the bottles beneath her knees and feet. This effectively stopped her shaking, and when she had finished the drink he lay her back on her pillow, smoothing the damp hair back from her brow.

'There! Better?'

She nodded, her eyelids already heavy from the unaccustomed emotion as well as from the rum.

'Good. Stay there till you're sent for.'

He left her, striding out of the cabin without a backward glance. She turned her face into her pillow, aware of a pain that had nothing to do with her freezing. Why had he simply put her away from him in the shower, when he must have known...*did* know...that she neither could nor would have prevented him from taking her? Was he so indifferent to her? She acknowledged, drearily, what she had been at such pains to deny to herself before. She was frightened of him, in awe of him—and she loved him. A picture of his face in the moment before he kissed her, the feel of his hands caressing her wet body, these things would remain burnt into her mind for ever, she was sure.

It had never occurred to her before that a woman could feel desire, physical desire, for a man's lovemaking. Now she knew that she wanted the skipper's caresses. Yet, oddly, she was *still* afraid of him, still unsure! And worst of all, he had made it clear from the start that she could be his mistress or his galley boy, and to be his mistress was a punishment, not a reward. If he took her, he would despise her, cast her aside when the trip was over.

She tossed and turned in the narrow bunk unable to find peace for her mind or her aching body. It was so unfair! She could not put on pretty clothes for him, use perfume, set her hair in the deep, natural waves into which it fell when freshly washed, because that would end the masquerade. She thought bitterly that she was going to be the loser whatever happened, for he would never love her and she was denied the opportunity of trying to attract him.

I wish I'd never seen the ship, her mind cried out, even as her heart denied it. Whatever happened, she could not regret the voyage, nor the love which had blossomed in such an unlikely place as a distant water trawler. And then it occurred to her that she knew nothing about him—he might have a wife and six children in Grimsby for all she knew!

The thought made her so miserable that she cried herself to sleep.

She awoke because somebody had switched the light on. She sat up rubbing her eyes, feeling very much better, and Taffy's black face met her gaze, poised at the edge of her cabin door, looking oddly disembodied, as well as anxious.

'You all right, Frankie? The boss told us you'd been frozen. Lucky you are he looked out when he did, else you'd likely be dead. The hot water can get the blood going if you're lucky and quick, and seems the boss was both. But you'd best get up now, if you feel fit, and give us a hand.'

'Yes, I'm fine.' Frankie scrambled out of bed, quite surprised to find herself fully dressed, and pulled on her boots, miraculously saved from the frozen deck and clean and dry once more. She dragged a comb through her hair and walked over to join Taffy in the corridor. 'Did someone sort out my other things? The duffle's rather important.'

'Aye. Jammy got all the stuff clean and dried. Your coat's on its usual hook. Now we'd best cut along to the galley and get a solid snack and 'ot drinks for all.'

'Okay.' She shook her wristwatch, held it to her ear, then grimaced. 'It's stopped. What meal is this?'

'High tea, I reckon. No one had time for dinner. Whilst you was snoring we got ourselves into a rare pickle. Not more'n three hours ago we hit a growler, just a small iceberg. Not even a direct collision, more of a brush. But it holed the hull.'

Frankie's hand flew to her mouth.

'Taff! Are we sinking?'

They reached the galley and entered the room. Taffy turned to grin at her.

'Do you think I'd come along and watch you shove your sea-boots on if we was sinking? Course not! But water's gettin in, and we're drawing much more draught than we should be. Weight of ice, see? So the skipper's got all hands on ice-clearance 'cep' for two, who're down in the hold with the busun, trying to plug the leak.'

'Ice! Yes, I remember the deck was iced up when I got frozen. Has it got worse?'

For answer, Taffy whistled and rolled his

91

eyes heavenwards, then went over to the stove and moved the boiling kettle to one side.

'Scrambled eggs, I think. You break the eggs, tiddler. As for the ice, you can see for yourself when you take this lot up to the bridge.'

'The bridge? Oh!—Couldn't I do the mess deck? Or take it up to the quarter deck?'

Taffy glanced across at her and grinned.

'Skipper give you a good hiding, did he? Told me he had, when he got you in the shower? Well, boyo, you deserved it and that's the truth, but you'll find the old man won't bear a grudge. Fancy leaning on a froze-up rail though, watching the black frost come up from the waves!'

'Oh, was that black frost? It hovered over the waves, I'd never seen anything like it before. Taffy, freezing's the worst thing that's ever happened to me I should think, it was like being turned to stone and then, when I began to thaw, it was agony!'

Frankie chattered on, but her horrified mind had absorbed yet another unpleasant fact. It had been bad that the skipper should have unfrozen her in the shower, but suppose he had not been the first to notice her predicament? It was clear from Taffy's placid acceptance of the captain's treatment that anyone, Spick, or Jammy, or the wretched Chuffy, would have treated her just the same.

She cringed at the thought of her own embarrassment and their stunned surprise. And as for what might have happened as a results, it was just too dreadful to contemplate!

'What's up wi' you, Frankie? You've gone red as a beet and you haven't stopped gabbing for five minutes! Get up to that bridge before I put my boot behind you!'

As soon as Frankie appeared on the bridge however, she realised that her fears were groundless. The captain treated her exactly as he had always treated his galley boy.

'Scrambled eggs? How on earth am I supposed to eat them and keep the helm? Oh, give them here!'

He reached for the scrambled eggs, sandwiched between two thick slices of toast, and took an enormous bite. He was alone on the bridge because the engines were merely idling, holding the ship head to wind, and his main task was to keep her helm steady and to watch out for icebergs which might drift into their vicinity. But it was a clear day, the picture on the radar screen good, and there seemed little chance of trouble coming from that direction. Frankie, who was standing beside him, holding his mug of coffee ready for when he required it, looked out of the window—and gasped.

The ship was almost unrecognisable. The ice was thick everywhere, long, dagger-sharp icicles hung from the rigging and on the boat-deck not a vessel could be seen, though Frankie guessed that the irregular humps in the ice must be their escape craft. The deckies were everywhere, oilskins frosting as she looked, hacking desperately away at the ice with axes, picks and sometimes, with their boots. And this combined attack was being partially successful, for even as she watched, Jammy and Chuffy, working on the whale-back, freed a gigantic slab of ice and sent it careering into the sea.

'A bit more off, and the hole plugged, and we'll move.'

The captain's voice was soft; casual, almost. Frankie glanced at him, wondering whether he was addressing her or merely thinking aloud. His eyes were fixed on her face, with an expression in them she could not identify.

'It isn't dangerous, then?'

One hand gripped the wheel, the other took her wrist. He turned her hand over, palm up, and drew his finger across the soft pads of flesh beneath her fingers, and round to her wrist. Her colour rose and she felt a pulse jump madly in her wrist. He, with fingers now firm on the pulse, felt it too.

'Not as dangerous as being shut in a shower cubicle with a naked woman. I wanted to...'

94

Behind them, the door crashed open and Tom's head appeared.

'Skipper, the hole's plugged. We oughter move. The lads say the worst of the ice is cleared.'

For answer, the skipper reached for the telegraph. It rang for slow ahead and with a promptitude which showed how anxiously the chief and his men must have been awaiting the signal, the engines roared into life.

The captain finished his coffee and handed the mug to Frankie as Tom strolled over to take the wheel. As he passed the galley boy he grinned cheerily.

'Up and about again, lad? Well, that's something you won't do again! Reckon the skipper taught you that, eh? You won't be sitting down for a week!'

Frankie gave him a desperate glance, crimsoned to the roots of her hair, and bolted from the bridge. The bosun grinned widely at his captain.

'Well, Boss, it's easy to see you warmed his little backside for him. Never seen a lad move faster! He's a good worker though, none better Taff says, and seems to like the life. Reckon he'll sign on next trip, and he'll grow steadier. Any road, a paddling never hurt a lad!'

The skipper was staring down into the radar, and it occurred to Tom for the first time that there was a stain of darker colour on his cheekbones. It would be worry, of course, because of the ice and the leak in the hull. He didn't show, much, the skipper, but it stood to reason that a man in command must worry!

5

The ship continued to stream north through increasing cold and ice clearance became a daily task. It was hard work, but not the most discontented deckie ever complained, since clearing the ice was as essential to survival as breathing. If the ship was not cleared and the weight of ice was allowed to increase there would come a time, the captain had explained quietly, when she would just turn turtle, taking them all to their deaths without any hope of reaching the boats.

But down in the galley, life went on much as usual. There were meals to be prepared and served, cooking to be done and washing, wiping up and clearing away. Dolly Parton had to be fed and kept active yet not allowed to escape and Frankie had perfected her rubbish disposal technique. Much to the amusement of the crew she always took the bucket out now when a clearance party were at work, and they said that her swift progress to the rail, the continual jumping and leaping as she tipped the bucket, and her subsequent race back to the quarterdeck, was as good as a play.

'Any one would think the deck was red-'ot, not covered with ice,' Jammy said, grinning. 'You look like a flea on an 'ot tin roof.'

But Frankie infinitely preferred being teased to being frozen stiff.

One night, when she was on late, she took the captain's hot drink to the officer's cabin where he was sitting in an easy chair, alone, reading a book. Matthew and the mate were on the bridge and Dodger was running a book on when they would trawl.

Frankie crossed the cabin, swaying as the ship's bows seemed to rise at an angle of forty-five degrees, and then continued her walk to his side. He glanced up, then closed the book and reached for the hot drink.

'Thanks. Been on the bridge?'

'Yes. Matthew and the mate are on watch. And the radar's working.'

It was a perpetual, nagging worry with the crew, she knew. When they were on deck they kept an eye on the mast as it turned and when they were below they checked every couple of hours, looking in to the bridge with some laconic remark—but eyeing the radar screen whilst they did so.

A dark eyebrow lifted quizzically.

'Quite a little mariner!' She smiled uncertainly and he gestured to a chair. 'Sit down, for God's sake! I'm not going to eat you.' He grinned, a challenging look on his face. 'Or anything else.'

She sat. She had learned quickly that one jumped to obey this Skipper, however one might treat others!

'Tell me about yourself.'

She shrugged, uneasy at the implications behind the question.

'Nothing to tell, sir.'

'Nonsense! Why haven't we had the police on the radio, demanding that we return to port with our precious cargo?'

'No one knows where I am, sir.'

The mobile brows lifted in pretended surprise.

'No? They wouldn't put two and two together and guess you'd run away to your young man? If they did that, knowing he was on board the *Atlantic Glow*, the authorities would soon put the right interpretation on the facts, wouldn't you think? Surely your parents...'

'I'm an orphan. No one's precious cargo.'

He drained his coffee mug and she jumped up, going over to collect it, happy to be able to escape from his catechism. But he caught hold of her wrist, pulling her to stand against the arm of his chair.

99

'So you're an orphan, but there'll still be explanations. What'll you tell your boyfriend? Won't he be annoyed when he finds out where you've been?'

She shook her head.

'No, it isn't like that, Trevor's more like a brother, I think. I've known him all my life.'

She knew, as she said the words, that she was speaking the truth though she had not realised it before. The affection which she had for Trevor was sisterly, with not even the shadow of the turbulent emotion that the skipper's lightest touch awoke in her.

'I see.' She saw that he was smiling and wondered what she had said which was so amusing. 'And the relations you live with? Won't they want to know?'

She turned her candid gaze on him.

'I used to live with an aunt, but I shan't go back. She doesn't want me.'

'Then what will you do? I don't imagine you'll sign on as a galley boy again!'

She sighed.

'I couldn't, could I, it wouldn't be fair. What will I do? Well, Trevor said I could be a waitress. Or work in a shop, perhaps? I expect I'll find something.'

He sat still for a moment, his eyes on her face, his expression inscrutable. Then he got to his feet and turned towards the door.

'I'm sure you'll find something. Now I'm going to do some work.'

She stood in the middle of the cabin after he had left, holding his empty mug tightly in both hands. He simply did not care what became of her. He could have promised her a good reference...no, he could scarcely do that! But surely there must be some way in which he could help? A captain must know people, have influence!

She walked towards the door. Perhaps he would ask his wife to find her work! The thought was a physical pain, so that she stood still for a moment, eyes closed, fighting it. Just to imagine another woman in his arms hurt, worse than being frozen on deck, worse than having her fingers shut in the car door, a remembered childhood disaster. Then, abruptly, she opened her eyes and, ignoring the galley, marched resolutely along to the mess deck.

She flung the door open. Chuffy was sitting there, feet up on the table, reading one of his rude magazines. He glanced up as she entered, his face very red and shiny.

'Chuffy, is the skipper married?'

'Naw, of course not. Who'd have *him?* With a temper like that a gal 'ud have to be desperate!' Chuffy smirked, then resumed his reading.

Frankie promptly marched out again, dumped the dirty mug in the sink and went to her cabin. She undressed and crawled into her bunk, knowing peace of mind at last. Ever since the thought had first occurred to her, she realised, there had been a little germ of uneasiness in the back of her mind. Now Chuffy of the rude magazines and the nasty practical jokes had eased that worry, at least.

She must not forget, she reminded herself, that even though he might not be married that did not mean there were no women in his life. She snuggled the blankets up round her ears. Even a crumb of comfort was better than no bread, she thought confusedly as she fell asleep.

'Wakey wakey, tiddler! Come on out of it!'

Frankie sat up and glanced at her watch. It was barely three o'clock in the morning, she should not have been called until six-thirty. She listened, but outside the wind still howled, and the pitch and toss of the vessel, to which she had become accustomed, was no better and no worse than it had been when she went to bed.

A clattering of boots outside the door brought her onto her feet. She dragged on her clothes and boots and made her way into the corridor. Luke was running along it, hop and go one, pulling on his second boot.

'Luke, what's happening? Why was I called?'

'Go you to the galley, boy, and git the kettle on.' Luke's rich Norfolk accent was comfortably rural. 'We're a-going to shoot the trawl.'

'Oh! Has the storm eased, then?'

He grinned at her, squeezing past.

'Good joke, that! Git you a move on!'

Hurrying into the galley, Frankie almost trod on Dolly Parton and swore softly beneath her breath, then bent and picked up the comfortable bundle of feathers, bringing the bird close to her face.

'Daft old hen! Get back in your box, it's the middle of the night!'

Dolly was becoming a very domesticated creature, Frankie reflected, putting the bird back amongst the wood shavings. She waddled around the galley when they were cooking, getting under their feet, begging for scraps, putting her head on one side to see what they were doing and uttering the most affectionate coos.

Presently, with the kettle boiling merrily and an assortment of food spread out on the galley table so that the men could help themselves, Frankie had leisure to think. She did not think it usual for a galley boy to be woken when they shot the trawl, or not from what Taffy had told her, so she supposed that she had been specially woken to serve the bridge. She poured two mugs of coffee, therefore, and made her way to the bridge. She opened the door, closed it softly behind her, and then, halfway across the floor, froze into stillness for a moment. Like the radar. The beam of light was motionless!

The skipper was leaning out of the window shouting instructions to the deckhands and the sparks was at the helm. Heedless of the coffee, slopping over the mugs onto the good bridge carpet, Frankie hurried over to the skipper.

'Sir! Radar's stopped, sir!'

Outside, the arc lights illuminated the wedding-cake of the iced-up deck, throwing into relief the black figures of the men scurrying about, and in the dark sea the aluminum floats of the trawl looked like pearls on a necklace. It was a violent sea still, and noisy. The captain obviously did not hear her small voice against the scream of the wind and the crashing of the waves.

Burdened with the coffee, Frankie made a long arm and reached out to give the sparks his mug. Then she tugged at the skipper's sleeve.

'Sir, please the radar...'

He turned so quickly that he sent her and the coffee flying. He compressed his lips, grabbed her off the floor like a rag doll, and thrust her against the window.

'Quiet!'

He turned to scan the deck narrowly, then bellowed 'Hook on!' through the open window. Frankie watched. Only when the bosun had indicated that the trawl was all set, did the skipper turn to Frankie, impatience in every line of his face.

'Yes? How many times must I tell you...'

'Radar's stopped, sir.'

He gave her a quick glance, then crossed to peer incredulously into the hood.

'By God, so it has. The devil!' He chewed his lip, then turned to Sparks, holding the wheel level with some difficulty. 'Take care, man, you're sailing blind!' He turned back, opening his mouth to give Frankie an order, then snapped his fingers. 'Curse it, you've not got your duffle. Never mind, stay there.' He had closed the bridge window but now he opened it again, and leaned well out. 'Wally. Wally! He pointed to the radar mast, then bellowed, 'Two men on the whaleboat to keep a look-out,' and slammed the window shut. 'Where's my coffee?'

'You knocked it out of my hand. I'll get you another.'

When she returned with a fresh mug of coffee he was alone, standing at the helm. He took the mug, drank, then glanced automatically at the radar and swore beneath his breath, an ugly little curse that made Frankie blink.

105

'Sparks has gone below to see what he can raise on the radio. If there's a ship anywhere in the vicinity with radar still working we can get advance warning of any bergs in the area, for instance.'.

As he finished his explanation, the door opened and Sparks' head came round it.

'Can't raise anyone, sir.' The sparks was a red-headed young man with a pale, freckled face which blushed easily. He glanced at the captain, hesitated, then spoke out. 'You're going to continue trawling, sir?'

The look the skipper shot at Sparks was glacial.

'Of course. Need I remind you that we're here to get fish and not for the good of our health.'

Sparks, scarlet-faced, muttered something and disappeared again and the captain turned to Frankie, still standing with her nose pressed to the glass, gazing out.

'Am I going to continue trawling! I suppose you'll ask me whether I think it's safe!'

Frankie turned round, blinking as she tried to accustom her eyes to the darkness of the bridge after the brilliant beam of the searchlight outside.

'No I shan't. You're the boss.'

The simplicity of the remark made him reach out and rumple the soft hair at the nape of her neck.

'True. And I'm trying to catch fish! Is your sight good?'

She turned back to the window, peering out.

'Yes, I've got very strong long sight.'

He was holding the wheel steady but he put his hand out again and touched the nape of her neck, making a small shudder ripple along her spine. She longed to turn into his hand and into his arms, but she knew better than to do so.

'Will you watch with me? The men on the bows will shout back, or wave, if they see a berg, but it's tricky out there in those conditions. We may see it first.'

They did. After no more than fifteen minutes' peering, some trick of their searchlight's beam flung small rainbows cliff-high before them. Frankie clutched the captain's arm. 'See? A *huge* one!'

He swung the wheel, then flung open the bridge window to its fullest extent as Jammy, at the bows, turned and made his hands into a megaphone, screaming, 'Dead ahead, dead ahead, dead ahead!' and then charging precipitately for the bridge door. He tumbled in with Dodger close on his heels. They were both blinking into the darkness like startled owls, for constant gazing into searchlight's beam made the sudden dimness of the bridge seem like black night.

107

'See it, Skip?' Jammy wheeled round and stared. 'Ah, you did! She's on the port bow, going past, I hope to God!'

'Right lads, now go back to the bows. Not to watch again, we saw it before you as it happens, but just to make sure we're clear of it.'

They left the berg behind, their trawl safe, and presently the deckies went to get some sleep until they were needed for the haul. Frankie stood by her post. There would be no dawn to gladden the eye or the heart, but she remained because the captain wanted her to do so, and she found comfort in even such a frail sign of need.

The haul when it came, was poor, the weather conditions appalling, especially without the radar. Yet they continued to fish, and to steam north.

There was a hatch between the galley and the mess deck, through which Taffy, with considerable dexterity, slung food on to the crew's hopefully extended plates. The officers, however, were always served by the galley boy, either on the bridge or in the officers' dining cabin.

Today, as Frankie entered the room with a jug of soup, she appeared to have interrupted a less than amiable discussion.

'...drift ice can be dangerous, but the radar's working again so we'll continue to steam north...'

'We'll hit the polar cap,' the mate interrupted, looking at the captain across the table, 'which won't help much.'

'We might see it, perhaps.' The Captain glanced at Frankie. 'What sort of soup is it?'

'Tomato, sir. Tinned.'

'I'll have some.'

The meal progressed with no further conversation. All the men disapproved of the decision to go further north, Frankie could see that, but the captain was determined. Eating, however, continued with great concentration, for the men were all large and needed the energy the food provided.

The mate's spoon scraping his pudding dish clean reminded Frankie of her duties. She collected the dirty crockery but, before she could leave the cabin with it, the mate stood up and called her back.

'Frankie, I'm on watch, so bring my coffee to the bridge. Skip can have his in here, the others'll fetch their own.'

Frankie went off to fetch the coffee jug, amused by the remark. It was plain that the men had found the silent meal uncomfortable and did not intend to prolong it over coffee! She served the watch first, then returned to the officers' cabin, where the skipper sat in solitary splendour.

'Coffee, sir?'

'Please. When I've drunk it I'm going out to see how the deckies are getting on with clearing the ice. Want to come?'

Her heart skipped a beat. If he wanted her company then it must mean he liked her! Oh, not in the way she wanted him to like her, perhaps, but any crumb of affection was a comfort. She nodded vigorously.

'Yes, please. I'll get my duffle.'

Together they walked to the bridge, where he donned his oilskins and sou'wester. He looked rather disapprovingly at her though, when she returned to join him a moment later.

'Haven't you got a frock?'

'A *what?*'

He grinned, and she caught a glimpse of what he must be like ashore. She could imagine him grinning like that over some small, shared joke, holding hands with a girl, kissing her.

She dispelled the image quickly. He was speaking, serious once more.

'A frock, lad. This!' He tugged at the shiny black oilskin he wore and she realised why it was so named. It had no fastenings as a coat or jacket might but was simply pulled over the head like a frock.

'Oh, that! No, I don't think so.'

He caught her arm and pushed her into the galley.

'Taff, didn't Spud have a frock?'

Taffy, taking five minutes off with his eyes closed and his feet up on the kitchen table, crashed into a standing position, eyes still half closed, body at an angle.

'Yessir, yessir!' there was a pause. 'What did you say, sir?'

The captain sighed, but repeated his question patiently. Taffy wrinkled his brow in thought.

'He must have, sir. Reckon it's on the mess deck, hanging by the calendar. Fetch it, Frankie.'

Frankie, returning with a somewhat muddy oilskin, pulled it down over her head, then added her muffler.

'That's better.' The skipper looked approvingly down at her, though his lips twitched. She guessed that she looked absurd in this huge, tent-like garment. 'Now if you get caught by a wave at least you won't freeze into a block of ice, like Lot's wife.'

She accepted this without scepticism. She had seen too much now, to underrate any of the stories the men told. Only yesterday she had seen a gannet, wings raised for flight, fall frozen on to the boatdeck. Now that she knew about the Arctic, she guarded Dolly

Parton from the outside as zealously as the men did.

Up on deck, the men chipped desultorily away but when they saw the captain, axes swung with more vigour and two men who had been sheltering on the whaleback came guiltily out and began to work again. The wind was fierce, blowing voices away before one could catch the words that had been spoken, but the skipper leaned down and put his face so close to Frankie's that she could feel the warmth of him through the mufflers both wore.

'See the drift ice? That's why we shan't shoot the trawl here.'

She followed his pointing finger and saw that the sea was littered with floating ice, small bergs almost, though only a few feet across. Then she exclaimed, catching at his arm.

'Look! On the ice! Oh, the darling!'

A seal lay on a slab of ice like a girl sunbathing, its face turned towards them, eyes huge with curiosity. He nodded, then caught her wrist and pulled her back to the quarter-deck and into the warmth of the companionway. He shut the door, unwound first his muffler and then hers, then sat himself down on the stairs, pulling her down beside him.

'Frankie, a man would never say 'Oh, the darling' like that! Fortunately, I was the only one near enough to hear, but you must be careful.'

Frankie blushed.

'I'm sorry. But you know, I wouldn't have said it to anyone but you. It's because when I'm with you it's sometimes hard to remember I'm a boy.'

He stared down at her, an arrested expression on his face.

'It is? I find it hard, too. I can only think of...'

He caught hold of her, their oilskins squeaking and their knees colliding, and his mouth found hers. It was a brief, harsh kiss, made ridiculous by the quantity of clothing between them, the narrowness of the companionway, the sou'wester dripping icy water down on to Frankie's face. He moved away from her, then drew his forefinger along the line of her lips.

'God above, how I want you! But I'm going to chop ice for a bit, instead.'

He got up and returned to the deck, leaving her still sitting on the stairs feeling shaken and starry-eyed. That kiss had said a lot. Or perhaps she had read a lot into it, she told herself, as she made her way to the mess deck to shed her oilskin.

He *had* said he wanted her! Could a man want to make love to a woman without feeling some sort of affection for her? She shrugged the frock off over her head and chided herself crossly for uselessly supposing. They had an agreement; so long as she kept her secret and did her job to the best of her ability, he would keep the pact. If he held her in any sort of esteem, then perhaps, when the voyage ended...

At the thought of the voyage ending, however, her mind sheered away. she could not bear to think about it, knowing that there would be other voyages, when the *Artic Glow* would sail without her. Thinking of him, facing the dangers without her, month after month, sailing into the endless night, the bitter cold, gave her a faint echo of the pain she would feel when it happened, at last. When he had long forgotten her.

She returned to the galley to find Taffy sunk in slumber in his chair, chin on chest, snores reverberating around the small room. Roosting on his knee, for all the world as though it was her natural perch, sat Dolly Parton, eyes closed, beak sunk on soft, billowy breast.

They're happy enough, Frankie thought enviously, getting out the flour, sugar and shortening. Neither of them has silly urges which make them miserable, and I must keep mine under control or I'll ruin my life. She began to bake.

The captain chopped ice all afternoon. When Frankie took coffee to the bridge she saw him, in the arc-lights, hurling himself into the work, barking orders at the men, sweat streaming down his face despite the bitter cold. She could see, too, that whatever the reason for his deciding to join the men might have been, his presence was having an excellent effect on the work. The ice was noticeably less, the whaleback and the area around the radar mast clear and the boats were appearing for the first time for days. She had heard sufficient horror stories on the mess deck to realise that under Arctic conditions, boats would not help survivors for long if they were wrecked unless the accident took place in a heavily frequented part of the ocean, but nevertheless, she was glad the boats had appeared again.

Jammy came into the galley at tea-time to give her a hand since Taffy was having an hour off, and talked with animation of the captain's prowess with an axe.

'Like the mad strangler of Clapham, he is,' he remarked, taking one of Frankie's tea-cakes and biting into it. 'I wouldn't like to argue with 'im with an axe in his hand!'

'Don't you mean Lizzie Borden?' Frankie objected, putting a dozen tea-cakes under the grill and setting the butter nearby. 'What was that rhyme? Lizzie Borden took an axe, and gave her father twenty whacks.'

'And when she saw what she had done, she gave her mother twenty-one.' Jammy chuckled and peered into the cake tin. 'Is that cake for today? If so, I'll start slicing it.'

'How kind! Well, don't eat too much. Has the skipper come back down yet, or is he still on deck?'

'He's on the bridge. Look, I'll take the cake and butter into the mess and you can hand the hot tea-cakes through the hatch to me. I can hear the men tramping in. And you can pour the tea as you usually do.'

Tea was the only meal of the day which the galley boy was expected to cope with by himself, whilst the cook had a rest, and Frankie rather enjoyed it, especially since Jammy or one of the other hands usually helped out. Now, she moved over to the hatch with the big teapot and put it on the serving shelf.

It was then that she missed Dolly Parton. Puzzled, she looked in the bird's box, beneath the table and up on the pipes which ran round the ceiling of the galley. Dolly often roosted up there when the movement was fairly smooth. The bird was nowhere to be seen. Frankie poked her head through the hatch.

'Jammy, did you see Dolly when you were in here?'

Jammy, sitting on the table swinging his legs and eating cake, shook his head.

'Nope. I don't remember seeing her.'

'Oh, lord! Suppose she got out?'

She ran out of the galley into the corridor,

and then, heart in mouth, up the companion-way which led on to the quarterdeck. The men had been coming down after ice-clearing, the door might well have remained ajar for several moments. If Dolly had gone out there...

She pushed open the door. Not two yards away was a bundle of grey feathers and a pair of pathetic pink, stick-like legs, the toes curled in death.

She should have closed the door quietly on the little corpse and gone below to grieve. She should never have shot out on deck, bending to pick up the bird, never hearing a roar of horror from the bridge, heedless, in that moment of danger.

The killer wave, forty feet high and curled at the crest like an avenging claw, death in its translucent depths, raced towards the *Artic Glow*. The skipper hurled the bridge door open and clattered across the quarterdeck, towards the small figure on its knees with the dead bird clasped in its hands.

The sea won. It reached Frankie, knocked her head-over-heels along the deck, the cold of it robbing her of breath to cry. It snatched the dead bird from her loosened clasp, hurled her against the rail. It froze as it ran out of the scuppers, forming new diamond necklaces, new spiky white sugar castles. But Frankie saw none of them.

6

Frankie came to herself to find she was in her bunk surrounded by hot water bottles, and covered with a great many blankets. She opened her eyes and frowned round. Her sheets had been stripped from the bed and lay in a heap on the floor. What on earth had happened to her? She could remember running out and kneeling to pick up poor, dead Dolly and then nothing. Absolute blankness. No whisper of her experience had remained with her to haunt her dreams.

Presently, she turned her head. The captain was sitting on the edge of her bunk, reading. He looked angry, his brows drawn close, his lips in an ominous line. For a moment Frankie seriously considered pretending to be asleep still. Then, with a sigh, she spoke.

'Skipper? What happened?'

He turned towards her, but there was no warmth in his glance. His eyes were scornful, flicking over her without either concern or interest.

'You went on deck without a coat, to pick up a dead bird, and a killer wave got you.

118

You're bloody lucky to be alive. Whether we're so lucky to have you remains to be seen. All you are is trouble.'

The words, spoken with cold conviction, cut like a knife. She felt her lips tremble and turned her face to the bulkhead so he would not see her distress.

'I'm sorry, I didn't...'

'Sorry! You're trouble, I tell you! I left the bridge, the wheel, everything, to get you in! As luck would have it, Raker came in then to ask about the next watch, and grabbed the helm, otherwise God knows what could have happened. The weight of the sea knocked you head-over-heels, it could have capsized us with no one at the helm! If you'd been a boy, I'd have beaten you!'

She stared up at him, suddenly seeing the injustice of his remarks.

'Are you saying you only went out because I'm a girl? Is that it? That you wouldn't have done the same for Jammy, or Chuff?'

He paused, then looked away from her.

'They wouldn't have taken a risk like that.'

'Jammy might. He's only the deckie-learner, after all.'

He sighed and stood up, looking down at her. His expression was difficult to read.

'I'd have gone for any of them. That's true. But I'd have called out, got someone to take the wheel—because it was you I just ran.' He

119

bent over her, seizing her shoulders, hauling her upright in bed. 'And what *good* are you? You're still more child than woman, though you've got a woman's body which I can't forget, no matter how hard I try! If you were older, more experienced, you'd be in my bed by now—and willingly too, by God! As it is, what good *are* you?'

She stared straight into his angry eyes. The touch of his hands on her shoulders was sending shivers through her, she longed for tenderness from him, for his kisses. But she knew where that would lead, he made it obvious enough! He would take her as his mistress and then cast her aside when the voyage was over, despising her for her weakness. As, indeed, she would despise herself.

'I'm a good galley boy.'

Her small voice sounded smaller after his furious tones. He stood up, releasing his hold on her shoulders. She crept beneath the blankets, watching him uneasily. Then, after what seemed an age, he nodded slowly.

'You are. Taffy says one of the best. So *be* a galley boy, for God's sake. Don't make things difficult for me.'

'Me, make things difficult for you? I don't know what you mean!'

'No? Who put you in the shower when you froze to the rail, and refrained from seducing you? Who brought you in and stripped you and wrapped you in blankets today? Every action like that means I have to see you're a woman, because I can't allow any one else to touch you!'

Shame and fury struggled for supremacy; fury won. She shot upright in bed, clutching the blankets above her breast, and glared at him.

'If you find the sight of me so distasteful don't damned well look at me! Don't do anything for me! I daresay if you'd just chucked me on the bunk and covered me in blankets I'd have survived. And a lot you'd care if I didn't!'

'Care? Damn it, Frankie, I'm a man short already, I don't fancy making it two! Anyway, I've a responsibility to my crew. I signed you on, I'll get you home. Alive and well. If I'd not stripped you—do you suppose I *enjoyed* tearing iced and soaking clothing off an unconscious girl?—you'd probably have died.'

'Right. I'll try not to nearly get killed again. And now get out of my cabin!'

She knew she'd gone too far as soon as the words were out of her mouth. He was halfway to the door but he checked, then came back like a tornado. He plucked her out of her blankets and put one foot up on her bunk. Before she had caught more than a glimpse of his intentions she was upended across his knee, his hand coming down on her rear with the

121

force and regularity of a steam-hammer.

'You *dare* speak to me like that! Have some respect!'

It really hurt and she fought back, but not too violently. Perhaps whacking her would get some of the anger against her out of his system and anyway, too much wriggling might well lead to disaster. She was clad in a long, white shirt, certainly not her own property, and a pair of light tan summer-weight slacks, also a great deal too large. So insecure did she feel, in fact, that she grabbed the waistband of the slacks as she was hoisted from the bed and still gripping it firmly when he administered one last, stinging slap and stood her on her feet. They glared at each other. He was breathing hard, his nostrils flared, his lips compressed.

'What do you say?'

It was like a parent chiding a child, she thought resentfully. But she knew he was right. He had just saved her life, no matter how reluctantly, and anyway she should never have ordered him out of her cabin, not on his own ship. She hung her head, then jerked her chin up and stared straight at him, colour still staining her cheeks.

'I'm sorry I was rude, Sir.'

The afterthought of the last word made his eyes lose a little of their chill but he just said curtly: 'Good. I'll have no more of it.'

Then he turned and left her, standing in the middle of the cabin in the outsize shirt and slacks, looking after him.

'Skipper wallop you?'

Taffy's enquiry was only mildly interested, and Frankie nodded sulkily.

'Well, it served you right. Running out on deck in this weather! Could have been your death. You all right now?'

Another nod.

'Good. Then you can serve the officers' supper.'

It would have been nice to act just like a girl and shout, 'No I won't, he's a beast!', Frankie thought, meekly taking the big dish of toad-in-the-hole down to the officers' cabin. But the boy she acted so faithfully would never have behaved like that. Frankie, the galley boy on board the *Arctic Glow,* was a sensible lad who would take his punishment like a man and not bear a grudge. And anyway, it was not the spanking that stung but his remarks. His insinuation that she had engineered the wave which knocked her unconscious so that he would be forced to undress her! Worse, his remark that he had not enjoyed the experience one bit! She gritted her teeth, remembering with most vivid clarity the look on his face in the shower, when...She gripped the edges of the dish so tightly that her knuckles whitened. He was altogether hateful, he most certainly did like looking at her, in fact he had wanted to do a good deal more than look!

She tapped perfunctorily on the officers' door and opened it. It was safer to think about his hatefulness rather than the other things. She must remember that in the days to come.

Two of the engineers were in the cabin, and the sparks and the captain. The chief looked hopefully at her dish as she entered.

'What've you got, Frankie? Sausage and mash?'

Mr. Ferguson had noticed the sauce bottles wedged together on the serving board, no doubt!

'Better than that, sir. Toad-in-the-hole. I'll bring the mash in next, and there's baked beans.'

She served, taking good care not to catch the captain's eye. Heaven knows what he might read into a friendly glance, she thought defensively, still sore from their recent encounter.

When the meal was finished she left the men to talk, with a jug of coffee on the table between them, and returned to the galley. Taffy was a little concerned over her, she could tell, and kept glancing at her.

'Lad, why did you come back to work? Skipper said you could stay in bed till tomorrow breakfast.'

Pride had got Frankie dressed and down to the galley, but she was feeling the strain already, and it probably showed, she thought ruefully. Not that she ever looked nice now, not in Spud's horrid, ragged clothing.

'Would you mind, Taff, it I went to bed now? I was upset over the things the skipper said to me, that was why I got up. But I really am tired.'

'You look it. Wash the salt off with a good, hot shower and then get a good night's rest.'

'Yes, I will.' She hesitated, a question suddenly popping into her mind. 'Taffy, why didn't the skipper shove me under the shower, like he did last time?'

'Deckies had just finished ice-clearing. The showers was full. You weren't frozen, mind, just bruised and wet. Off with you, lad.'

Frankie made her weary way to the showers in a thoughtful frame of mind. Could that have made him angrier—because he could not push her into a shower and let one of the men bring her round, as he undoubtedly would have done had she really been a boy? Then, shrugging, she entered a cubicle and shot the bolt across. It was no use wondering, it was best to forget the whole episode!

Emerging some twenty minutes later with

seal-wet hair and a clean and comfortable body, Frankie re-entered her cabin in a much better frame of mind. She went over to the mirror, and stared at her reflection. A small, oval face, large, dark blue eyes with thick and dusky lashes, the hair darkened by water and slicked back. She sighed. What wouldn't she give right now for a box of scented talcum powder and one of those swansdown puffs! And some eye make-up—just to play around with. She was wrapped in a dull, brown towel, too, and she shut her eyes, visualising a dream dress—it would be pale gold organza with a darker gold sash. She would have filmy tights, sandals with the thinnest of gold straps and the most precarious of pin-heels. She would set her hair in waves and curls all over her head, and...

She opened her eyes and her glance fell on the sheets, still in a heap on the floor. She began to smile. Why not? Why not pretend, just for a little while, in the privacy of her own cabin? She thought about bolting the door but decided against it. Only the previous evening she had listened to a horrific story told by Raker about a man who had locked his cabin door and had subsequently knocked himself unconscious when he fell from his bunk during a storm. No, she wouldn't bolt it, but she would push her box of clothing against it. That would prevent anyone bursting in on her too quickly.

First and foremost, she would fashion a dress. But from what? Cabins did not run to curtains or frills. Her eyes fell on the sheets, and she remembered her first idea. She picked one up and then heaved Spud's box out from beneath the bed. His clothing, fortunately, was covered with safety pins. She collected a handful, picked up the first sheet, and began.

Ten minutes later she had fashioned herself an evening gown with a brief bodice and a swathed skirt which she thought was rather good. She added to the illusion by pinning a corsage above her left breast. It was not really a corsage of course, it was a blue hankerchief of Spud's, but turned and twisted and pinned, it really looked convincing.

Her next task was her hair. It was still damp and already it was beginning to curl. She pushed it with her fingers, fashioning it into artful, natural waves. When it was dry she combed it carefully, then went and stood in front of mirror.

She smiled guiltily at the young lady who looked back at her. She put her chin up haughtily, standing as models stand with one leg forward and one hand on her hip. Yes, there was no doubt she made an entirely convincing young woman, which wasn't surprising, when you considered...

The sound of the door opening behind her took her completely by surprise. She swung round, her fingers flying to her mouth, to see the skipper, a jug and two mugs in his hand, gazing at her unbelievingly, his mouth dropping open. But it lasted for tenths of a second only. A scowl descended. He shut the door and slid the bolt across, then put the jug down on the floor.

'Where the devil did you get that dress? Are you mad?'

She came out of her dreams with a bump clutching at the sheet, half afraid he would rip it off her back, so thunderous did he look.

'I-it's a sh-sheet off my bed. I w-wanted to see if I could still l-look like a woman.'

She expected him to be furious, to berate her soundly, for after all, she had run a hideous risk now that she thought about it. But he no longer looked angry. His eyes roamed over her, taking in the golden-brown curls, the low cut "gown", the way it clung to an obviously feminine figure.

He crossed the room, eyes still on her.

'You look all woman. It's a miracle to me that even in jeans and sweaters no one's suspected. Has anyone ever told you you're beautiful?'

He said it matter-of-factly, but it set her heart pounding.

'No. It w-wouldn't be true.'

He took hold of her by the hips, pulling her nearer him. His eyes darkened in the way she remembered.

'Do you realise that if I went to that door and called one the men, the cat would be out of the bag? And you, my dear little girl, would be fair game?'

His eyes were on her breasts, clearly outlined through the thin sheeting. His hands moved on her hips, subtly caressing. She swallowed.

'Yes. But it wouldn't be fair, would it? You wouldn't really do that to me?'

He pushed her away and turned to leave the room.

'No, it wouldn't be fair. I brought you hot coffee with your dram of rum in it. Goodnight.' His hand was on the doorknob when he turned back. He looked at her, letting his eyes travel from the tip of her head to the top of her toes and back again. Slowly. When his gaze was steady on her face once more she was scarlet, half convinced that the sheet must be transparent. 'Frankie, is *that* fair?'

Before she could speak he had turned and left her, shutting the door firmly behind him.

Next day, soon after breakfast, they shot the trawl again. It was a good thing, Frankie reflected, running at everyone's bidding. If there had been awkwardness between herself and the captain, he needed her help too much to let it weight with him and soon they were back on their usual footing. He barked his orders, she leapt to obey them. He never insinuated, by a word or a look, that he remembered her femininity and she was careful to be Frankie, the galley boy, and to stick to the part.

She enjoyed watching the haul and knew it was a time when an extra person on the bridge was a help, so turned up there when the men tumbled onto the deck to raise the trawl. Later, she was glad she had not sulked in the galley.

She stood in her usual station watching as the commands were given and instantly obeyed, the trawl broke surface and swung out of the sea—then stopped. The mate had bawled in a voice that cracked, at the winchmen to stop and the skipper, leaning out of his window, whipped round so quickly that he nearly knocked her over, and grabbed the megaphone.

'Ware mine, everyone, ware mine. There's a mine in the trawl!'

Frankie watched, horrified. She could see it clearly now in the light from the searchlight, swinging evilly in the netting, booming resoundingly once against the ships side. A live mine, which could go off at any moment and blow them all to kingdom come!

The mate, armed, incongruously, with a mop, was trying to fend the mine off whilst the bosun leaned out as far as he could and endeavoured to cut the net with a pair of shears. Every now and then the entire ship's company froze to stillness as the mine swung and boomed, hollow and wicked, against the *Arctic Glow's* hull.

'Sparks, keep her on course and keep her slow! Frankie, keep watch. I'm going down.'

The skipper reached for his oilskin and sou'wester and then slammed out through the bridge door. Frankie watched him arrive on the lower deck, lean over and examine the mine, then tie a length of rope round the nearest bollard.

She knew at once what he meant to do. He was going to try to climb down the rope, with a wild sea running, and cut the mine free. She knew some of the risks inherent in such a mad act, guessed there were more.

'No! NO!' She had spoken aloud and was unaware of it, not noticing the sparks' curious glance at her. 'It's too dangerous, he shouldn't...'

'He's the boss, lad.'

'Yes, but how should we manage...' she

could not go on. Then, even as the captain turned away to say something to the mate, Chuffy grabbed the rope, knotted it round himself beneath the arms, and climbed like a monkey over the side.

It was difficult to see what was going on, but there was a moment when a shout of anxiety rang out, then a cheer, and then the trawl came up, empty, spilling a few fish back into the water where they lay, flapping feebly, whilst the men brought Chuffy up. The skipper caught Chuffy in his arms as if he had been a child and carried him across the quarterdeck. He flung open the bridge door and tipped his burden gently on to the carpet.

'Rum, quickly', he snapped, holding out a key, and Frankie ran to the bond cupboard and brought back a full bottle of rum and the crew's dram glass. He snatched it from her without ceremony, splashed spirit into the glass, and supported Chuffy's head, holding the glass to his lips. The mate, who had apparently stayed to see to the lashing of the trawl, arrived on the bridge and went straight over to the cupboard where the first-aid box was kept.

'Do I look at him here, Boss, or shall we take him along to his berth?'

Chuffy had gagged over the rum and then swooned, it seemed to Frankie and now he lay inert, his eyes closed, his colour drained.

'We'll take him to his berth. Frankie, you bring the first-aid stuff.'

The two men lifted Chuffy's inanimate for with great gentleness and took him along to the double berth he shared with Jammy. They rolled him out on to his bunk and then the mate gingerly began to undress him.

'Is he frozen?' Frankie asked the skipper.

'No. His leg got crushed between the mine and the ship.'

The mate, it seemed, knew what he was about. He had to cut Chuffy's thick serge trousers off, though, and when the leg was revealed at last Frankie shut her eyes for a long moment.

The calf muscle had been almost torn off and there was blood everywhere but as the mate said, it could have been a lot worse. The shin bone was bruised, but so far as they could tell, neither cracked nor broken.

'I'll sew it up, Skip. I'd best. There's disinfectant, and then I can dry dress it with that antibiotic powder. If we leave it like this anything could happen.'

'Right. You can do it?'

The mate pulled a face.

'I've never treated a wound like that, but there isn't much choice. Guess if I can mend a net I can mend a muscle. Pass me the stuff, Frankie.'

Frankie, pearly-faced, threaded the curved

needle for him and then stood well back. His first attempt, however, brought Chuffy round with a strangled shriek which made all three of them jump. It occurred to the Skipper at this point to try an anaesthetic of a sort.

'Go and fetch the rum bottle,' he ordered Frankie, holding out the key again. 'Run!'

She ran, knowing that with every minute that passed Chuffy was more likely to regain complete consciousness. And presently, she handed bottle and glass to the captain, who ignored the glass but held the bottle straight against the patient's lips. The spirit glugged and Chuffy swallowed, and when he'd had almost a quarter of the bottle the skipper laid his head back on the pillow. His forehead was lightly beaded with sweat.

'Phew, that should keep him out for a bit!'

Without asking, Wally leaned across, picked up the bottle and took a swallow.

'Dutch courage. Want some, Skip?'

'I shouldn't need it. You're the one who's doing the embroidery!'

But this proved only half true. The wound was cleaned with antiseptic, dried to the best of the mate's ability, and then the stitching commenced. But it was a long and tedious job, and before he was even halfway, his hands were shaking with the strain of the task and with his efforts to hurry before Chuffy gained consciousness again.

'I'll take over,' the skipper said at last. He picked up the bottle and drank, then dribbled another dram or two into Chuffy. 'You go and see what's going on above, Wally.'

The mate left them and Frankie held Chuffy's leg still and watched as the tiny stitches crept round the gaping wound, closing it as efficeintly as was possible. Several times the Captain stopped his work and rested his hand, took another swallow from the bottle and then returned to his work, but at least it was finished. He stood up and stretched, his face worn and anxious.

'There. He should do, now.' He handed the needle to Frankie, who doused it in antiseptic and replaced it in its small case. 'Look, Taff'll have to manage without you for a bit. Move your stuff into this cabin; Jammy can sleep in yours for a night or so.'

'Me? Sleep here? But wouldn't he be better with Jammy?'

The captain yawned and stretched, looking down at her, his eyes mocking.

'He'll need someone with him twenty-four hours a day for a bit. Can you mend net, honey? Can you wrestle with the trawl in conditions like this? I'm two men short now, because of this accident, and I don't intend to make it three. This is why we carry a galley boy, dammit!'

She went and stood directly in front of him,

her eyes pleading for understanding.

'Chuff may be able to hear you, you know! Look, I *can* mend the net, though I'm slow. I'll stay with him willingly of course, but couldn't I just do the day-shift? Or just when Jammy's busy with the trawl?'

He seemed to be enjoying her discomfiture. He put his hand on her shoulders and rocked her gently from side to side, looking down at her through narrowed lids, his eyes gleaming.

'No. Don't you fancy a hermaphrodite role as male nurse?' He laughed and pinched her chin unnecessarily hard. 'Well, you'll just have to lump it, honey, because you're the nearest thing to a nurse we've got.'

The endearment frightened her because she sensed the sarcasm behind it. She remained standing before him, however, her eyes on his face.

'You know why I'm afraid to nurse him. If I'm with him all the time, sleeping in a bunk right by him he might...he might...'

'Guess? So he might!' The smile left his mouth and she saw the hunter gleam in his eyes. 'And if that happens, my dear little girl...'

'You wouldn't punish me for what would be no fault of mine? Would you?'

His hands bit into her shoulders, pulling her nearer, but she resisted, waiting for his answer.

'A punishment? That's damned insulting! You wouldn't suffer, honey, you'd enjoy it.'

He was so close now that his breath stirred her hair and suddenly she knew why he was behaving so strangely. She glanced across the cabin at the rum bottle. It was completely empty.

'Skipper, you drank all that rum!'

He shrugged.

'Guilty, ma'am,'

She shushed him desperately and he smiled, one eyebrow shooting up.

'In vino veritas, you pretty thing. Come here!'

He tried to jerk Frankie right into his arms and she kicked out, then punched him, desperately trying to bring him back to reality.

'Captain, if anyone comes in now, or if Chuff regains consciousness, the word'll go round that you're gay!'

That stopped him. He let go of her, a grin curving his mouth.

'By Christopher, the girl's right!'

'And what do you suppose they're doing on the bridge? They could have decided to turn south in view of Chuff's accident. What course did you set?'

It was nonsense, of course. Not one member of the ship's crew would dare change course without his consent, she was sure of it. But his smile faltered and a frown began to pucker his brow. Before he could recapture the initiative she bent down and handed him the empty rum bottle.

'Take this with you and throw it over the side quietly. I don't know how you managed to keep a steady hand with all that liquor inside you.'

He passed a hand across his brow.

'A miracle, isn't it? My head's beginning to thump like a steam hammer. I think I'll get some black coffee from the galley.'

'That's a good idea.' She held the door open for him. I'll give the mate a call if Chuffy wakes in much pain.'

She closed the door behind him when he'd gone off in the direction of the galley, leaned against it, and breathed a long sigh of relief. That had been a very close shave indeed!

7

For forty-eight hours Chuffy was so ill that Frankie had little time to worry over anything except his health. It speedily struck her, however, that painful though the leg wound was, it was not responsible for his high temperature and sickness. He must have caught a chill from being suspended above that wicked, freezing sea for an hour or so and then he must have got an infection. On the morning of the second day, in fact, when she lifted him to drink, she heard, like surf pounding on a distant shore, liquid bubbling and growling in his lungs.

She dressed his leg daily with considerable care, ignoring his shouts. Once, a heavy hand hit her across the head, making her see double for a moment. She looked up at him, eyes watering.

'What did you do that for?'

'Because it *hurts!* Damn you, let the mate do it.'

'He can't, they're busy. We're two hands short now, because you're not fit.'

He whimpered as she touched the wound,

139

but it was cool, and the knowledge that if it was going to turn septic if would be hot to the touch made her very conscious of its temperature when she cleaned it and puffed the antibiotic powder into the ragged slit.

Soon after this, the captain popped his head round the cabin door to suggest that he take over for a moment whilst she spoke to Sparks about the possibility of getting medical advice from somewhere.

It was an excellent notion, and they were fortunate in contacting a Russian icebreaker with a doctor on board. The sparks reeled off Chuffy's symptoms and, at the doctor's request, the mate produced the first-aid box and once again, to Frankie's dictation, Sparks repeated the contents of the box.

The reply, when it came, was very helpful. The Russian doctor thought the treatment they were using on the wound would prove effective, but said the man must not use the leg too much. When he heard of the fever which racked the patient, he advised tepid baths, and plenty of cool liquid to drink, followed by ice to suck. Then, when they read out the names of the drugs in the box, he told them that one was, in fact, an antibiotic which could be taken internally if mixed with water. He suggested a dose, wished them luck, and Frankie prepared to carry out his treatment.

Her first call was to the bridge. She did not feel she could give Chuffy a tepid bath without a good deal of assistance since he weighed at least twelve stone, even in his weakened condition. However, she chose a bad moment for her request. She walked on to the bridge, her rehearsed speech ready, to find the captain and the mate obviously having an altercation of some sort. When she spoke the mate turned away to gaze out on to the deck and the skipper faced her, impatience obvious in every line of his figure.

'I've spoken to a Russian doctor about Chuffy, sir, and he told me what to do and what medicine to give. But he said we were to give the patient tepid baths, and I can't lift him. Could you send two of the hands to do it?'

'Get Taffy. He'll help.'

He turned his shoulder on her, addressing a remark to the mate. The interview, if such it could be called, was plainly at an end.

In the event, her fears were groundless. Taffy was marvellous, lifting the young man like a baby and putting him gently into the zinc tub she had borrowed. They sponged until the skin temperature seemed to drop and Chuffy's incoherent mumblings changed to quiet pleasure in the coolness and comfort of the water, then they dried him and lifted him back into his bunk where he lay, propped up with four pillows, blissfully sucking ice cubes.

Two hours later, he was so obviously improved that she suggested he might take some blancmange, and though he only managed two spoonfuls, he admitted that he had enjoyed it.

By evening, when he had three doses of the medicine inside him, he was almost talkative, in a lazy, lethargic sort of way. As she bustled round his cabin, taking her time over the tidying so that she could provide the company he needed before going to help Taffy in the galley, he watched her, throwing out the odd comment now and then.

Into this comfortable scene. Chuffy, all unknowing, proceeded to throw dynamite.

'Why do you go so red so much, tiddler? When you and Taff were bathing me you were red as a beet.'

'Was I? Well, you're heavy.'

'You didn't lift me. When I was a kid I suppose I blushed, but...' he stopped speaking and stared at her. 'When I first came round after the stitching, was it *you*...' his forehead creased with the effort of remembering. '...didn't the skipper call you honey?'

She could not prevent her face from burning, but she made a brave attempt at nonchalance.

'If he did, he must have been teasing—he

drank nearly half a bottle of rum, you know! Here, take this medicine.'

She carried the bottle and spoon over to his bedside and held it out to him. He caught her wrist and pulled her nearer, easily despite his weakness.

'By God, you're a girl!'

She laughed, then pushed a curl back from her forehead. It was an unconsciously feminine gesture.

'Me? Chuffy, you must be very ill indeed! Do let go of my wrist.'

She read his intention in his eyes and jerked herself free, knowing she was blushing again but powerless to stop herself.

'Don't mess about! Take the medicine.'

He leaned over and picked up the bottle and glass, his face knowing.

'So I was right, you *are* a girl. If you'd been a boy you wouldn't have looked so sick, nor jerked yourself back from me. You'd probably have landed me one, mind.' He poured the medicine into the spoon. 'Well, who'd have thought it of the skipper, and him such a hard case! Just wait till the others hear.'

Frankie had retreated from the bedside but now she returned, sitting down on the edge of his bunk and fixing pleading eyes on his face.

'Chuffy, you wouldn't tell? The skipper

didn't know anything about it until I gave myself away one day. It was too late, then, to turn back, so he said if I did my job well and didn't get found out he'd not take any action. *Please,* Chuff, don't tell!'

He grinned at her, shaking his head slowly.

'Oh my, what a temptation! But I won't say a word, Frankie, because you've looked after me a treat. when I think how I slapped your head, and...Oh my *Gawd!*'

He looked so genuinely horrified that she guessed at once what he was thinking about. She chuckled.

'That tattooing? It could have been worse!'

He nodded, scarlet-faced.

'By gum, so it could!'

They sat in companionable silence for a moment, both reviewing their new knowledge. Then Frankie spoke.

'When I said don't tell, Chuff, I mean't don't tell Skipper as well as the other deckies. It's vitally important that he doesn't know I've been rumbled. You won't let on?'

'Course not. Too damned sticky for everyone, you wouldn't be able to act natural, and...No, I won't say a word.'

'Chuffy, you're a sport. Thanks!' She gripped his hand tightly for a moment, then stood up. 'In a way it's a relief that someone else does know. And now I must go and do some work for Taffy, or he'll throw me off the ship!' She hesitated. 'Chuff, you're a lot better already, would it worry you if I went back to my own cabin, and Jammy came back here? I'm *not* worried, honestly, but it's a bit of a strain.'

'No, that's all right, I'll be fine. And I won't say a word to Jammy.'

'Skipper? It's ten to seven.'

Frankie watched him stir and wake, rubbing his head violently as he sat up. He took the hot tea from her and raised a brow.

'Chuffy better? You back in the galley?'

'Yes to both. He was so much better that I moved back to my own quarters last night. His temperature's normal now and he'll be sitting up in a chair later today. He manages pretty well now, so I'm back in the galley.'

He sipped his tea, eyeing her as he did so.

'Well, well! And you had no trouble with him?'

She knew what he meant and smiled primly. No need to lie!

'No trouble at all, Captain. Have you finished that tea?'

'Nearly.' He drained the mug and handed it to her. 'Don't fail to come to the bridge after you've served breakfast. There's something I'd like you to see.'

'Yes, all right. Breakfast's in ten minutes.'

As soon as breakfast was washed up and cleared away, she went up to the bridge. The captain was already there, conning the ship, with Sparks at the helm. Seeing the young man there she knew they were probably going to shoot the trawl quite soon and felt mixed emotions. The last time they had hauled, the mine had been in the Cod End. She remembered it as a malignant thing, rolling over and over in the waves, no doubt waiting for its next victim. But that was not the only reason she felt her heart thump doubtfully over trawling. As the skipper said, they were here for fish; they must get a good catch or his reputation and, presumably his job, would be lost. But as soon as they had full fish-rooms, they would turn for home. She dreaded the return to port, when she would have to leave the ship—and the skipper— and make up her mind what course her life was to take.

'Frankie? Here.'

She obeyed his gesture, walking across the dimmed bridge to stand by him. It was pitch dark outside, as indeed, it would be at noon.

'See that white line? There, see?'

She gazed, then gasped, looking up into his face.

'Is it land? Is it?'

'We-ell, it's the pack-ice. Somewhere, it joins the land. We'll go closer.' He glanced at the radar screen and then, sharply, at the echo sounder. 'Are we on a shelf, or ... By God,

146

I think it's a shoal! Get the men up, we'll shoot the trawl.'

In ten minutes the trawl was over the side and the ship had slowed. A heavy sea was running and as they neared the edge of the ice Frankie saw why the skipper had wanted her on the bridge. As the beam of the searchlight dipped and curtsied with the ship's motion they could see penguins, seals and walrus, some lying on small floes, others congregated on the edge of the pack-ice, for all the world like spectators come to watch a football match.

She laughed delightedly, pressing her nose to the glass.

'Isn't that wonderful! Look at the huge, fat old walrus, trying to scratch himself behind the ear, and him so gross he can scarcely bend at all!'

They were within a stone's throw of the ice now and their lights were attracting a good deal of notice. Hundreds of pairs of eyes followed them as they moved along.

'That's close enough. Hard over, Sparks.'

Sparks began to move the wheel as something occurred to Frankie.

'Skipper, you know when the trawl brought that mine up?'

'I'm not likely to forget it!'

'No. But when the mine was cut free, quite a few fish fell back into the sea; they were alive, flapping like anything. But they didn't dive down and disappear, the way I thought they would. They just sort of died!'

He nodded.

'That's right. The trawl had brought them above their natural swimming level in the depths. Their balance, if you like, had been destroyed and they were too light to get back down.'

'So that's why! It sounds crazy, of course, but lots of things sound crazy out here.' She squeaked, clutching his arm. 'Look! There!'

His eyes followed her pointing finger.

'You mean the polar bear? Yes, I hoped we might see one. We spotted a big fellow yesterday, floating by on a floe just like someone catching a bus, but you were with the invalid, I couldn't get you up here just for that. Look at the size of the creature!'

She nodded vigorously, her eyes devouring the sight she might never see again. The polar cap, the walrus, the great white bear, as different from the yellowing, despondent polar bears in the zoo as chalk from cheese.

'Sparks, put her over. We're still too close to the ice.'

Even in the bridge he had to shout above the noise of the sea as it crashed and mumbled against the massive ice-cliff, polishing it to opal and agate as the searchlight swung across.

'I have, Skipper. She isn't answering.'

In a moment·the Skipper was at the wheel, all his attention with his ship, and she knew herself forgotten.

'Bring her over! Come *over,* you cow!' He stopped hauling on the wheel and jumped for the telegraph. He rang for full astern and slowly, far too slowly for comfort, the *Arctic Glow* began to back away from the suddenly menacing pack-ice.

'Rudder damage?' guessed the sparks.

'I don't think so.' The captain looked disquieted, nevertheless. 'Currents, probably, pulling hard so she couldn't answer at once. We shouldn't have gone so close in, we'll get clear now, and steam for the open sea.' He turned to Frankie. 'All right, tiddler, you've seen all there is to see. Go back and help Taffy with dinner.'

Later tipping a pile of chipped potatoes into smoking fat, Frankie told Taffy about the animals on the ice—the walruses, the penguins, and the towering polar bear.

'It made me miss Dolly Parton more than ever,' she admitted rather wistfully. 'I'd love a baby seal, or a bird. Something to take care of.'

'Good job you wasn't close enough to grab one,' Taffy said thankfully. 'You're looking after Chuffy; be content with that! Got a pet at 'ome, have you?'

'I used to have a terrier called Nip. But he was run over just before I came aboard.'

'That's hard,' Taffy sympathised. 'Why not get yourself another, when we dock? They're good company dogs, better than people, some think.'

'I would, but I've got nowhere to go.' She glanced up, to find Taffy eyeing her shrewdly. 'I daresay you guessed I ran away from home, but it wasn't really home. Just an aunt who took me in five years ago, when my parents were killed. Charity, I suppose you'd call it.'

Taffy sniffed.

'Cold, charity is. You've a place here now, boyo, and I hopes you know it. You need never lack a berth whilst I'm cook aboard this ship. And if it's lodgings in Grimsby you're after, there's half-a-dozen I know who'd take you in. I'm a single man myself, but Raker's married and his missus takes a lodger or two, and there's a nice little pub in Cooper's Lane where they've a bedroom for trawlermen, nothing posh, but it's clean. To say nothing of Jammy's Ma; she'd welcome you. Especially now she's only got Jammy to watch out for.'

'Oh? Is his father dead?'

'Oh aye, died out here years since. But it's his brother I'm meaning. Jammy had a brother called Alfie, only a year or two older than our lad. His ship got run down by a liner, in mid-

Channel. Alfie wasn't one of the lucky ones. Broke his Ma's heart, Jammy reckons.'

'That's dreadful. Why does Jammy stay?'

Taffy shrugged, dipping cod in batter.

'What else is there for him to do? Besides, he's got the sea in his blood, same's me. But I reckon she'd welcome you, for her son's sake.'

'Poor woman. I've heard several of the deckies talking about fathers and uncles who've died out here. It really is dangerous, isn't it, Taff?'

The cook transferred the dripping fish to the pan and shouted his reply above the sizzling.

'It is an' all. Hardest work in the world. The death rate amongst trawlermen is four times higher than amongst coal miners. Reckon a quarter of the men you've bunked with this trip will die at sea. Eventually.'

She felt her heart sink; why must she fall in love with someone whose career was so fraught with danger?'

'Just for fish! Just for something to eat with chips! It seems wicked, Taff.'

'Aye. Hardest, coldest, wickedest job in the world. Yet I know why we do it. Do you, laddo?'

Frankie thought of the companionship, the good food, the money earned. It did not balance the dangers and difficulties. She had

151

seen the deckies with her own eyes, working for twenty-four hours at a stretch, barely shutting their eyes before they were ordered out on deck again.

'You couldn't know, not after half a trip. Two day millionaires they call us, when we're in port. A good haul means a good percentage, see? Then a quick spend, and we're off again. Back to the cold and the danger, and the feel of the Arctic wind on your cheek. We're a team, yet we work for ourselves. Get it?'

'You mean independence?'

Taffy nodded, turning his fish in the hot fat.

'Aye, partly. On trawlers you can work every trip or miss a trip or two. Most just talk of missing, but they're signing on when she's ready to sail. They can make big money sometimes, other times it's just the rent. But *you* make it! Salvage, if you're lucky, can give you enough to retire on. It's a bit like doing the pools, or backing the 'orses. Uncertain.'

'I suppose I do know what you mean. But what about Jammy? His poor mother!'

'Jammy'll make skipper one of these days. That's another thing, most skippers started out as galley boys, or deckies at any rate.'

Frankie blinked. This was something she had never even considered!

'Really? Do you mean our skipper was once a galley boy, chipping spuds and being told off by everyone?'

Taffy chuckled and spooned some chips out on to a dish.

'They're done, get the dishes ready, tiddler. This skippers's a bit different. But he was probably a deckie learner, once.'

'Why different?'

But at this point Taffy's dinner reached perfection and he began to set golden brown pieces of cod, fresh as cod can be, out on to the dishes, then he leaned over and pushed together the motley array of sauce bottles for the crew to help themselves through the hatch.

'Cut along, before it goes cold,' he admonished, when Frankie showed a tendency to linger and repeat her questions. 'Get a move on, we'll be hauling in forty minutes!'

When she had served the officers, Frankie made her way to Chuffy's cabin and took his dinner to him. She had steamed him some fish and cooked potatoes in the steamer at the same time, then made a parsley sauce with dried milk. But Chuffy's face fell when he saw the unappetising plateful.

'Steamed fish? Aw, Frankie, how'll I get better on mush like that? Why not chips, I'm sure I smelt chips when you opened the door.' He reached over and buried his nose in the voluminous folds of her jersey. 'Yes, you've been cooking chips, I can smell them on your jumper!'

'I know, but you aren't well enough for...'
Frankie was beginning, when the cabin door
opened with a suddennes which caused both
of them to give a guilty start. Chuffy managed to hide his confusion by taking a quick,
disgusted mouthful, but Frankie, pulling
back from his bedside, felt her cheeks, crim-
soning. The captain walked across the cabin.

'Enjoying your dinner, Chuffy?' He turned
a penetrating glance on Frankie's flushed
face. 'I'll stay with the invalid now. You can
go back to the galley.'

'All right. I'll come back presently, Chuffy,
for your plate. If you eat it all up you can
have some pudding.'

'What is it? Ground rice?'

Frankie giggled.

'Egg custard. It's good, honestly!'

She closed the door on his disgusted exclamation and went back to the galley. When
she judged that he had had sufficient time to
eat his fish she returned to his cabin, to find
the captain there no longer and Chuffy's plate
empty. She gave him his custard, then decided that she would have an hour of peace
and quiet in her own cabin, reading on the
bunk. She had actually managed to borrow
a book from Matthew, who admitted that he
was a thriller freak, so now she settled down
with a vintage Ngaio Marsh and a handful
of saltines which she had nicked from Taffy's

store cupboard. Beneath her pillow was a hard, green apple, to eat when all the saltines were gone. She felt content with her lot.

She was well into her book when the door opened softly and the skipper slipped inside, then coolly shut the door behind him. She was immediately wary, feeling her heart begin to beat faster. She raised her eyebrows, trying not to sound defensive. 'Yes? Am I wanted on the bridge?'

He came over and sat on the end of her bunk without being asked. His eyes were very bleak, his mouth hard. He spoke without preamble.

'Keep away from Chuffy. He doesn't need you now.'

Frankie's eyebrows shot up. This was a complete *volte face!*

'I spend scarcely any time with him. I just go in to see to his dressing and to give him his meals.'

'Oh? Give him his meals, eh? I saw him pushing his face up against your breasts!'

'He was not! He s-said he could smell chips on my jumper, that's all!'

'Huh! Do you take me for a fool? He knows, I'd take my oath on it!'

'And you think I would let Chuffy...how *dare* you! I wouldn't...'

'You would! You're just playing hard to get

155

with me! Or do you prefer a young lout, reeking of fish...'

She forgot her fear of him and sat bolt upright, then slapped wildly at his face. Her fingertips caught his cheekbone and he grabbed hold of her, pushing her back on to the pillow. She saw jealousy flaming in his eyes, felt it in the savage kisses he rained on her face, her neck, then she was in his arms, held painfully tight, whilst his heart thudded against her slight breast.

'You're mine! Body and soul, whilst we're on this ship! If anyone has you, it'll be me!'

She shook her head stubbornly, refusing to listen to the voice which clamoured within her, telling her to give in, to let him possess her now; love would come later.

'I'm not yours, Skipper. I'm mine! I'm working my passage and you promised!'

He pushed her away, his expression savage.

'All right, damn you! Be independent while you can. Soon enough you'll lie under some lout who'll slap your face when he's drunk and give you a kid every year! If that's what you want, just keep away from me!'

He stood up, staring down at her from smouldering eyes. She knew a moment of such scarlet, blinding fury that she found herself on her feet not six inches from him, words tumbling from her lips without the slightest recollection of moving from the bunk.

'I hate you! I don't want any man! Just keep away from *me,* do you hear? I shan't run to you when I'm in trouble, and I'll lock this door every time I come through it. I hate you!'

She thought for a moment that he was going to strike her but he caught her shoulders, digging his fingers in, then shook her.

'Don't dare to lock your door! If anything should go wrong you wouldn't stand a chance.' She could feel his fingers tremble suddenly as he held her and his voice dropped its harsh, furious note. 'The rudder's damaged. Chiefie confirmed it just now. If you lock the door I'll break it down!'

She said nothing, staring straight in front of her at his white jersey and tightening her lips. He swore beneath his breath and then released her abruptly and strode over to the door.

'All right, hate me. Ignore me, if you must. But don't lock your door, Frankie?'

She looked across at him. He looked tired out and worried, and love won't go away for the asking; she felt her heart flutter in her breast and without thinking, put her hand over it as though to quiet its tumult.

'I heard. I won't lock it.'

He nodded and was gone, leaving her alone, aching from the pain of fighting him, having to deny him. Why must it be like this, she

157

thought miserably, sitting down on her bunk and picking up her book. Why must her heart want him and long for him, no matter how cruelly and harshly he might behave, whilst her head reminded her that to give in would be madness?

8

When the trawl came up, Frankie was not on the bridge to watch it. She heard all about it, though, when the men went tumbling down to the fishroom.

'What sort of fish was it? Was it a good haul?' she asked Jammy as he hurried past the galley.

'Good? Fantastic! Cod the size of you, tiddler, very near.' Jammy's tone was jubilant, his face wreathed in smiles. 'The old man's found this time, he really has!'

'That's great. I missed it, though. Busy in the galley.'

She hoped no one would think it strange that she had deserted her post on the bridge.

Jammy grabbed her arm.

'Come and take a look for yourself! Come on, Taff can spare you for a minute.'

She was following him along the narrow passageway when the captain came towards them. Jammy went straight on but she hesitated, then had to continue. He flattened himself against the bulkhead as she sidled past with lowered eyes and sulky mouth, but his very nearness dragged her eyes up to his face, the familiar rhythm quickening her heartbeats. For one second their eyes locked and she knew an absurd desire to confess her love. Then she remembered stories she had heard of explorers lost in the Arctic, of how they wanted only to lie down in the soft snow and sleep. But it was fatal. Those who succumbed never woke. It would happen to her if she gave way to her overwhelming urge to bathe in the warmth of his approval, let him make love to her! She would slide from love to the little death of his indifference, once they reached port.

She was almost past when he touched her arm.

'Help with the gutting. We're two deckies short.'

For a moment, she could have cried. There was she, thinking of love, and what was he thinking about? What did her closeness conjure up in that bleak, harsh mind? Gutting! Damned, dead cod!

Fortunately, at this point her sense of humour came to her rescue. She was alone with him in the passageway and she dropped a demure curtsy, tugging at her forelock as she did so.

'Oh yes, sir, with pleasure, sir! What a *kind* thought, sir!'

She saw his mouth compress and shot off

as fast as she could run towards the fishroom. He might have been going to laugh, but she was not willing to take any risks with a temper so uncertain as the skipper's!

And it turned out that she was not needed. She entered the fishroom to find the men standing ankle-deep in a heaving mass of silvery bodies. Some of them were still very much alive, she noted with inward horror. A great, ugly fish with an eel-like body and a spade-shaped head snapped like a bulldog at her boots and she jumped back. She caught the mate's eyes and raised her hands in a helpless gesture. Where did one start?

The mate's job was shelfing the best fish and now he put a great cod which must have weighed upwards of forty pounds carefully on the shelf he was filling and moved over to Frankie.

'Got a message for me, tiddler?'

'Not really. The skipper sent me to help gut.'

The mate stared for an incredulous second, then roared, a great bellow of mirth which made several of the deckies stare.

'He was kidding you, lad! You've got to know what you're doing with fish this size. Take your hand off soon's look at you, those big catfish would. You get back to the galley. When we need help from babes in arms we'll let you know.'

Considerably relieved, Frankie made her way back to the galley. She thought hopefully that it was a good sign when someone who had been very angry with you descended to pratical jokes. Or had it been a joke? Had he been trying to humiliate her? Or, worse, had he meant her to stay in the fishroom, learning to gut? What should she do?

On her return to the galley, she put the question to Taffy.

'A joke it was, boyo! No work for a stripling, that. No, no, I won't have my galley boy slipping and sliding around, covered in scales, with 'is fingers bit off, like as not!'

'I bet you wouldn't say that if he was in here,' Frankie observed, coming thankfully into the galley and shutting the door. Taffy laughed.

'Would I not? I'm not one whit scared of the skipper, tiddler!' he gave her a portentous wink. 'Good cooks ain't ten a penny! No one risks losing a master-chef like I am!'

'Oh, is that your secret?' She beamed at him, thankful to know that it it she was bullied for leaving the fishroom, he would back her up. 'What'll I do, Taff?'

'You make a big batch of scones. There's plenty of butter and if we serve 'em hot they won't last long. Yes, you do that.'

Standing at the table with the yellow bowl filled with scone mix, rolling, cutting and put-

162

ting the scones into the oven, Frankie was content. She had always enjoyed cooking and this sort of cooking was best of all. Not that she particularly liked making scones, which was a repetitive, unskilled sort of job. What she enjoyed was cooking for people who would genuinely appreciate her efforts. The deckies were her friends and made no bones about criticising her failures and praising her successes. They treated her with affection, as a sort of mascot, and this made the dullest cookery interesting to her.

Humming a tune as she moved from table to oven, with Taffy nodding off on his chair, she wondered whether, instead of waiting at table, she might not try to get work as a cook. In a school canteen, perhaps, or a cafeteria. But she knew it would be different. The atmosphere aboard the *Artic Glow* could be found only on a distant water trawler isolated from humanity, fighting for survival in the bitter tempests of the Arctic ocean.

She wished that she might have one more trip as a galley boy, just one more! Long ago, she had ceased to believe that Trevor would sail back to Grimsby and solve all her problems in a lordly manner. He could not, in any case, do so, because he no longer knew the extent of her problems. How to help someone who had fallen in love with a trawler skipper, a man who spent over forty weeks a year sailing the worst waters of the world, would daunt a far more ingenious mind than Trevor's. And besides, she did not intend to tell anyone. To suffer from unrequited love was a shameful as well as a painful thing, she decided. It isolated you from friend and enemy alike, until you could break the spell and fall out of love again. If you could.

She got a batch of scones, golden brown, out of the oven and put another lot in, then looked throughtfully at the fire. She really should bring more coal in. When she could persuade one of the hands to do this chore she did, because it was hard and dirty work, shovelling the coal into the long scuttle. Jammy, always hungry and extremely goodnatured, was always willing to cart coal in return for a handful of biscuits or a hunk of cold meat pie, but today everyone was busy and Taffy was asleep. She would obviously have to do the job herself or watch her scones fail to rise.

She was careful to wrap up warmly, however, since the coal was kept in a bunker on deck. She topped her warm things with the black oilskin, picked up the coal scuttle and set off.

It was cold on deck, the pounds slippery with scales and fish. She trod carefully, keeping her eye on the searchlight beam, remembering the killer wave which she knew had nearly made her its victim. The sea was very rough, but she could see no immediate like-lihood of a monstrous wave rising out of its depths.

Carefully keeping her back to the bridge, she opened the door of the bunker and began to fill her scuttle. She hoped that no one on the bridge had noticed her, but in any event, she was only doing her job. The big arc-lights were out though, and the small ones merely glowed on to the deck. With luck, he would not see her at all, going so quietly and un-obtrusively about her business.

She had the scuttle half-filled when the engines stopped. It came as a surprise be-cause it happened so rarely and she straight-ened, glancing around her. What was hap-pening?

The wind had been gusting straight into her face, now it was on her cheek, and she guessed that the ship had veered slightly, though the movement seemed jerky and un-certain. She remembered the captain's re-mark about the rudder, and then shrugged and bent to her task once more. It was no business of hers if the captain chose to cut the engines! She heaved the full scuttle off the ground, staggering slightly under the weight, and made for the quarter—deck door.

Halfway there, an appalling, booming bang hurt her ears, and even as it sounded the ship jerked horribly. Coal, scuttle and Frankie went flying across the deck as the bows seemed to rise right up into the air. Frankie careered down the deck on her stomach, still gallantly clutching the now empty scuttle, then grabbed a rail as she shot past, managing to arrest her undignified slither. What on *earth* was happening?

She could not resist glancing up at the bridge window. She could see the skipper, speaking to the helmsman, then shouting down the voice tube to Chiefie in the engine room. But the crisis, whatever it had been, seemed to have passed, and the ship was on an even keel once more. Frankie got cautiously to her feet, then glanced ruefully at the empty scuttle. All her hard work was scattered over the deck, she really ought to fill it again.

Still she hesitated. She did not like the feel of the ship. A day before, if she had been asked, she would have denied having any sort of affinity with the movements of the *Arctic Glow*. But now the ship felt sluggish and heavy beneath her feet. She sighed, then braced her shoulders. Whatever had happened, she needed more coal for the galley. She must refill the scuttle.

She turned back to the bunker, and noticed at once that the wind was stronger. She got right inside the shelter of the small, hutlike edifice, uneasily aware that whatever had happened, she was very sure it had chosen a bad time to do so. Sparks had talked, at dinner time, of bad weather coming their way. Blizzards, he had said. There had been suggestions about a change of course, but Sparks had been sure they could not avoid it whichever way they turned. And now there was no doubt in Frankie's mind that something was very wrong. The wind was getting up, the sea was rising, yet the ship lay at the mercy of both, with her engines stopped!

She filled the scuttle and went back out of the coal bunker. As she did so she felt the ship shudder again, almost as though she had been kicked by a giant. Then, in a sudden gust of wind the door on the coal bunker slammed shut with her inside it still, and the safety lock gave a final, definite click.

Her first reaction was one of annoyance. The sheer stupidity of her plight made her want to scream. She shouted, and the sound reverberated round the small space, but she knew it to be very unlikely that anyone else would hear her. It would be another two hours before the deck watch turned out to haul the trawl and though she was sheltered and in no danger, it was both uncomfortable and humiliating, sitting there on a pile of coal, trapped and helpless.

But she would not have to wait two hours, because Taffy would smell the scones burning

and come to her rescue. The thought of her
scones burning to cinders brought her crawl-
ing across to the door, to bash its echoing
metal with her fists. Nothing happened. She
picked up a lump of coal and attacked the
door with that, and in the middle of her lusty
thumpings, the engines roared into life once
more. She sat back and pushed her hand into
her hair. Then she said one of the worst words
she had heard the deckies using. It sounded
satisfyingly wicked. She said it again, louder,
two seconds later because she had remembered the reason for getting the coal in. It
was because the fire had burned low. And if
the fire burned even lower, as it would, the
scones wouldn't burn and Taffy wouldn't
awake to wonder where she was.

Frankie sat back on the coal and said her
bad word a third time. Louder. It failed to
give her any satisfaction whatsoever. At the
end of two hours' waiting, she would be freezing cold and thoroughly bored. In a reedy,
wobbling little voice she began to sing a sea-
shanty. Presently, one solitary tear tricked
down her cheek.

The confusion on the bridge when the engines
stopped was orderly, with the captain and
Sparks trying to find out what was happening, keeping the suddenly helpless ship head

to wind, trying to raise the engine room on the voice pipe.

'Dammit Chief, what's happening down there?' the skipper yelled into the voice pipe. 'Are you all asleep or something?'

He glanced towards the deck. Last time he had looked, Frankie had been staggering back towards the quarter deck with the coal scuttle giving her an amusing list to port. Now the deck was empty. She had obviously got into the companionway before the ship had struck. He turned to the sparks.

'A small ice floe must have hit us a glancing blow, too small and low to show up on the radar, that's why we bucked like that. But what happened down below I can't imagine. Look, nip down to the engine room, will you?'

The sparks went and was back almost at once.

'It's all right, Skipper. The engine cut out as we struck and Chiefie and Ern were knocked over. The voice pipe got disconnected but it's okay now. Chiefie says the engines will be roaring in ten seconds flat if you can hold her head to wind until then.'

'I'm doing my best.' The captain moved the helm and frowned out into the searchlight's beam. 'Don't like the look of those waves, it's my belief there's a storm coming—and fast. I'll feel a lot more comfortable...ah!'

169

The steady note of the engines interrupted him and he leaned across to study the echo. 'I hope the trawl's all right.'

'It should be.' The sparks peered out through the starboard window. 'But whether we'll be able to give it full three hours—ah, here comes the snow!'

It came in a blinding blizzard, in seconds locking the ship in its whirling veil, making the radar unreadable, freezing on to the windows of the bridge.

The skipper was aware, in the pit of his stomach, of a strong sense of unease. It puzzled and annoyed him. The ship was all right now, her head was into the wind and she was riding the increasingly violent sea buoyantly enough. Below, the men would be finishing the gutting and cook would be making huge pots of tea, buttering bread, putting out a cake, perhaps. He frowned down on to the deck, uneasiness growing. Was she all right, that wretched, tantalising brat who had fooled him into signing her on as galley boy? Alarm knotted in his stomach. He had taken his eyes off her for perhaps five or six minutes, and in that time anything could have happened! His common sense told him that the sea had not been unusually rough, and though the ship had veered and bucked when she had struck the floe it had only been sufficient to knock someone over, not enough to

170

throw them over the rail and into the sea. But the worry would not leave him. An irritating little prude she might be, with her constant steady refusal to give him what he was sure they both wanted, but she was in his charge. He must find out if she was all right.

'Sparks, take the wheel. I'll get a deckie to come up. I shan't be long.'

The galley was quiet when he opened the door. Taffy snored in his chair by the fire, a batch of scones lay on the table, waiting to be put in the oven. But the coal scuttle was not in its usual place and of Frankie there was no sign.

Fear dried his mouth. He took the companionway two steps at a time and burst out on deck, straight into the storm. Snow filled his eyes and mouth and he stopped taking in breath and tumbled back into the shelter of the companionway, cursing his own stupidity. To rush out like a novice would help no one.

Luke, coming back from the fishroom still in his trawling gear, found himself accosted by a taut-mouthed skipper with snowflakes thick on his dark hair and sprinkled across his navy sweater.

'Give me that oily, Luke. I'm going on deck.'

Stolid, unimaginative Luke was thinking about the good smell of scones which came drifting along from the galley because some careless person had left the door ajar. He handed over his oilskin and the thick, fish-stinking muffler, added, unasked, his sou'-wester, and continued on his way.

The skipper forced his way against the wind out on to the deck. He stood there for a second, blinded by the violence of the blizzard, getting his bearings. Of course she might be lying, unconscious, against almost any piece of the deck impedimenta, but he never hesitated. He made straight for the coal bunker, bent down and lifted the safety lock, and forced the door open an inch. As he did so he heard a small voice defiantly lifted in song. It came from within. Forcing the door wide, he bent and peered inside.

She was there, sitting on a pile of coal, the scuttle grasped defensively in one hand. The pale triangle of her face turned towards him and he saw, in the dim light, an uncertain smile light up her eyes and curve her lips.

'I'm glad you came! The wind slammed the door and locked me inside.'

He reached in and took the coal scuttle from her. Then he held the door wide despite the wind's desperate attempts to slam it shut.

'Out!'

She crawled past him and he saw that she was filthy from her sojourn in the bunker and that tears had made tracks through the coal dust. Despite himself, he softened a little. But he did not attempt to touch her as they crossed the wind-lashed hell of the deck and forced their way in through the quarterdeck door.

Inside, he pushed her down the stairs in front of him and once at the foot, handed her the coat scuttle.

'No doubt it wasn't your fault, it was the wind's, I've heard your stories before. You've been *told* not to go on deck unless someone else was out there.'

Her chin sank on to her indescribably filthy muffler.

'My scones needed...my scones!'

She set off down the corridor at a run, lugging the scuttle behind her, apparently forgetting that he was in the middle of reading the riot act to her. But he did not follow. He turned back to the bridge and halfway there, began to laugh. Poor kid, it must have been terrifying, to find oneself locked in the bunker whilst the ship reared and plunged, the engines cut out, and a blizzard suddenly blew up. There had been tears on her cheeks, perhaps, but she had been singing when he reached that door. And not a quiver in her voice! However furious one might be with Frankie, one had to admire her pluck!

9

Taffy's reaction to his galley boy's appearance had been peremptory, to say the least. He awoke to find Frankie bending over the oven, pulling out a batch of nicely cooked scones. She put them on the table and then transferred another tray to the oven. And then, turning back to the table, he lifted the first well-risen, golden brown scone on the cooling tray with his hands... Taffy leapt to his feet.

'Don't touch them scones!' he howled. 'Your hands, boyo!'

Frankie glanced at her hands and then flushed scarlet, putting them defensively behind her back.

'It's all right, Taff, just a bit of coal dust! I had to fetch more coal in for the stove you see, and...'

'Fetch it? You look like you've been digging for it! Look at yourself!'

She glanced down at herself, then up at him.

'I'm in a bit of a mess, aren't I? I'll wash my hands and then finish off the scones.'

174

He bounded across the kitchen and took hold of her by the scruff of her neck. Carefully, using the extreme tips of his fingers. No sense in both of them getting black as coal!

'You will not! You'll go straight to the showers and wash properly. *And* all your clothing. *And* your hair.'

'But I'm getting tea, and the scones...'

'I'll see to that. Get to those showers.'

Frankie sighed and made for the door.

'Sorry, Taff. All right, I'll clean up.'

Five minutes later, standing beneath the spray, she was glad Taffy had seen her before the other men. The humiliation of it! Getting shut in the coal bunker was just the sort of thing a stupid young boy would do and she was trying so hard to prove to the men that she was every bit as capable and self-reliant as they!

Fortunately, she always kept her clothes clean and dry, so there was no difficulty about a change. She put on her own jeans and Spud's navy blue jersey, then her boots. She slicked her hair back, thinking she looked every inch a boy, and made for the galley.

But despite the fact that the deckies had not actually seen her in her blackened state, they all knew about it, as she found out when she joined them on the mess deck with a large cherry cake and a knife to slice it with.

"'Ello-ello-ello, how's the pit pony, then? Didyer enjoy sitting in the coal bunker?'

'Fancy taking a nose-dive into that lot, eh, Frankie? Better'n the Arctic Ocean, of course, but a lot dirtier!'

'Aren't you witty,' Frankie said crossly, digging the knife vindictively into the cake. 'I couldn't help it, could I? I was only getting the coal in. Then some fool stopped the ship with a jerk and the door slammed on me.'

'Oho, he's blamin' Chiefie now!'

'Stopped the ship with a jerk! Very maritime!'

Chuffy had been carried in to share tea by two of his friends and now he grinned across at Frankie with a good deal of sympathy.

'Don't take the mick, fellers. Who rescued you, Frankie?'

Frankie glowered.

'Skipper did.'

There was a yell of laughter from the men.

'That blighter 'as eyes in the back of 'is head! Bet he gave you a rollicking didn't he, Frankie?'

'Course he did,' growled Frankie, biting into a wedge of cake. 'Not for getting shut in, but because I went out alone. Anyway, the galley boy's always in the wrong from what I've seen.'

'Hear 'im! Don't you know the first rule of trawling, Frankie? Captains are always right, mates are sometimes right, but deckies are never right.' Jammy, Spick and Chuffy chorussed the old saying and Spick added, with a grin, 'So it stands to reason that galley boys, bein' such low forms of life, are right fewer times than deckies.'

The joke had to be dropped, however before the jest had grown stale. The watch came through to tell them that they were hauling, despite there being another forty minutes to go.

'Cap'n says the weight of the trawl's bringing water in too fast—we were holed when that growler struck—so we'll ease her off until the storm eases. Unless we get a good haul.'

'He wouldn't shoot the trawl again because the haul's good if he thinks it dangerous and the ship's holed, would he?' Frankie enquired.

But apart from a shout of 'Just you watch 'im!' from one of the hands, no one else had time to answer her. Fishing gear was being dragged on, cigarettes stubbed out, the last dregs of tea drunk. In less than sixty seconds, Frankie guessed, she and Chuffy were alone in the mess deck.

'Well, ain't it gone quiet?' Chuffy marvelled. 'You going up to bridge to watch the haul?'

Frankie hesitated. Had his rescue of her from the coal bunker negated the things he

177

had said during their row? But the recollection of those cold, hated words were back, ice-burning into her brain. 'Keep away from me,' he had said. And she, every bit as furious, had promised to do just that. How could she turn meekly round and return to the bridge when to do so must seem a sign of weakness?

'No, I'll clear away. Besides, I hope they don't have a good catch, or he'll shoot the trawl again!'

'We're here after fish and he won't take us home till we've got them,' Chuffy pointed out. 'If they're shoaling here, now's the time to trawl.'

'Yes, but…Chuffy, why's the skipper so desperate to make a good catch? Is he always like this?'

'Dunno. I sailed with Meadowes last time and we were gettin' fed up with him, I tell you. Didn't give a hoot whether we found or not, so our percentage stank. This feller's got a reputation to make, I darsay.'

'But he's gambling with men's *lives,* Chuff!'

Chuffy's round face looked as cynical as it was possible for him to look.

'We gamble every time we come out here, tiddler. Now give it a rest and 'elp me back to my cabin.'

After she and Taffy had taken him back to his berth, she had to fight a strong impulse

178

to go on to the bridge and show the skipper that she had not meant the things she had said. But her recollection of his words was too strong, so she returned to the galley instead.

'We'll do a Yorkshire,' Taffy was remarking prosaically, when the door burst open. The skipper's glance roved the two of them, then settled on Frankie.

'You! On the bridge. Double quick!'

His voice was like a whiplash. Frankie flinched, coloured, then cast Taffy a guilty glance. The captain had gone already, she could hear his footsteps thundering back to the bridge.

She followed him towards the door, then turned to raise her shoulders at Taffy to show her helpessness.

'What can I do? I'll have to go.'

And on the bridge it was obvious, as soon as she glanced out on to the deck, why she had been called. The radar showed only a confused picture of racing, whirling dots and through the glass of the clear view window she could see that every few moments the decks were awash with great seas. The men were clinging to stanchions, winches, anything to keep them on their feet. And the ice! The water was freezing before it could escape through the scuppers, perhaps the scuppers themselves were frozen, and where the boat deck must surely be there was a mountain of pale, reflecting ice.

'You! Watch!'

No other explanation was needed. He thrust her near the open window but not directly in line with it and pushed the megaphone into her hands. She would warn the men of anything approaching in the searchlight's beam, because once they began to haul they would not be able to watch for themselves.

He gave the order to release the tow, bellowing against the gale. Frankie doubted whether the mate could have heard the words but he had seen the captain's mouth move, knew what the order must have been. The towing pin was struck from its place with one mighty blow from Raker's hammer and the haul commenced.

As always, the sudden release from the weight of the trawl in the water caused the ship to bound forward. But lurch, Frankie thought, was a better word on this occasion. The *Artic Glow* lurched into the waves and her bow, instead of rising joyfully to the crest, ploughed through a great greenback so that the men were waist high in water, clinging desperately to anything they could catch hold of, including each other. Wide-eyed, Frankie watched as Spick, huge and reliable, caught Jammy as he was dragged past by the ebbing wave, undoubtedly saving his life.

Yet not a man left the deck. The haul was completed, the Cod End released and the fish poured into the pounds. It was a good catch, the net bulging with fat cod.

There was a pause on the bridge, a pause that could be felt. Frankie looked at the sparks' face and read fear there; not fear of the weather; but of what orders the captain might give. She glanced out and saw, with immense relief, that the mate was ordering the lashing of the trawl. She had not seen a signal given but the captain said nothing, merely watching as the men performed their tasks as rapidly as the conditions allowed. Then they made for the safety of the companionway, slamming the door against the massive, frightening seas, to make their way to the fishroom to gut. It might be cold and unpleasant work, but at least it did not offer the hazards of the open deck.

The deck was clear in the arclights. Sparks turned to the captain.

'I'm off watch now, Skipper. All right if I snatch a few hours'?'

'Yes. I'm off myself presently, but I think the gutting will have to wait. I want an ice-clearing party on deck as soon as it's practicable. Go and tell Wally to put the men on a rest period. They'll be rousted out as and

181

when conditions clear a bit.'

When the sparks had gone Frankie dared a comment.

'Why isn't she breasting the waves, sir? She seems...heavy.'

He answered in a flat voice, without glancing at her.

'She *is* heavy.' Only then did he turn towards her. 'The weight of ice has grown so immense that there's a very real danger of her turning turtle. I can feel it. And so, it appears, can you.'

For a moment there were just the two of them in the small, dim world of the bridge. The lights were always extinguished when they shot or hauled so that visibility was better, leaving only the dim glow of the instruments. He drew her towards him, not roughly or suddenly but with a gentle inexorability which she accepted, allowing herself to stand against him, his arms around her waist.

'What can we do to stop it, Skipper?'

'Very little. The men will rest and when the storm eases we'll get steam hoses working. If only the rudder were fully operational! The trouble may come because she's not answering to the helm quickly enough. If she has to be put over too fast she could just slide under.' His arms tightened round her. 'Instant oblivion, Frankie.'

She thought about the things that made

life so precious to her; springy turf beneath bare toes in summer, the warm sea splashing hot skin, the taste of a jam sandwich when you were very hungry, a long drink of cold milk on a breathless July day. And his touch. The way his hair flopped across his forehead, the sight of his hands on the wheel.

'I'm afraid,' she said in a small voice. 'I try not to be, but I am. If only there was something we could *do!*'

He was holding her tightly now, and bent his head to kiss the side of her mouth with a tenderness which brought the blood hammering to her face.

'There is. Come to my cabin, Frankie, and at least we can be together before we die!'

She sighed, then relaxed against him and his lips continued the argument, though he said not another word. Hot and hungry, they covered her face with kisses, her neck, the exquisitely sensitive area around her small ear. She sighed and trembled against him, wanting to give in, to know at least the shadow of love before drinking the instant oblivion he had spoken of. When he returned to her lips there was no pretense left between them. Her mouth opened under his, a flowering of trust, and she kissed him back, admitting her desire as her hands crept up round his neck, pulling him closer yet.

He put her from him, weak and dizzy, as

a step sounded outside the bridge. Just in time. The mate and Luke came in, cups of hot coffee in their hands.

'What's the position, Skipper?'

That was the mate, his greeting far cheerier than his expression, which reflected the grimness she had seen, earlier, in the captain's eyes.

'Not good, Len. Look, I'm going to get some sleep; if conditions improve, call me. Just try to keep her head into the wind and remember that she can't answer quickly to the helm.' He gave Frankie a push. 'Cut along, brat.' He walked behind her to the bridge door and there, pausing, he lowered his voice still further. 'My cabin?'

He went back in to the bridge again and she stood in the corridor, her mind racing. What should she do? In his arms, surrender was only a matter of time, she knew that if they had remained alone on the bridge without fear of interruption, whatever the next few hours might bring it would have found them lovers. But now? To go to his cabin in cold blood and shed her boy's clothes, and let him possess her? She felt shame and fear fight with desire in her mind. What if he was wrong, and the ship did not turn turtle? Then there would be a tomorrow, in which she would no longer be her own woman. She would wake up and despise herself, even if he

184

did not. And it's me I've got to live with for the rest of my life, she thought forlornly.

She glanced at the bridge door. It was still closed. He would be giving her time to go to his cabin and prepare herself. She shivered. Horrible, to so cold-bloodedly seek physical satisfaction in the face of impending death! She could not do it! Resolute at last, she turned into her own cabin.

She removed her clothes, then clicked the light off and climbed into bed. Fear, she knew at once, would be her bedfellow. She would lie here, shaking, until she was woken next morning to get the crew's breakfast.

Part of her mind, the secret, guilty part she could not acknowledge, lay there waiting for him, expecting him to slip into the room, close the door and get into her bunk. If he did so, she could tell herself that she had been powerless to prevent his onslaught, that he had taken advantage of his power over her, and would suffer fewer pangs of conscience as a result.

But he did not come. The door remained closed, the light off. And at last, worn out, she slept.

It hardly seemed possible, she reflected next morning as she walked along the corridor with his early morning tea, that last night had happened. She wondered how he would greet her, but felt no qualms over entering his cabin. He could not pretend that she had denied him for he had not put her to the test, had not come to her, last night. In retrospect, she could not believe that he had expected her to meekly drape herself across his bunk and wait for him, he knew her too well. And she was sure that he would not have put the decision so entirely on to her. He had, perhaps, been testing her. If so, she had passed the test with flying colours.

Which is odd, since I don't feel proud or successful, she thought crossly, tapping on his cabin door. I just feel tired and let-down.

She entered the room. He was sitting on his bunk, fully dressed in the usual dark trousers and white jersey. It occurred to her that his clothes were always immaculate; surely he must be the only person on board ship who kept a white sweater white?

'Morning, Frankie. Sleep well?'

'Yes, sir.' She blushed, avoiding his eye. 'Your tea, sir.'

'Thanks. After you've taken the mug I'll get some sleep.'

'Sleep?' She was so surprised that her voice squeaked. 'Didn't you...?''

'No, I didn't.' His expression was bland. 'Oh, my intentions were of the worst, rest assured of that! I came back here, you weren't around, and then before I had a chance to come a-visiting the bridge rang down that the storm was subsiding. So I decided to join the ice-chipping party.' He flexed his shoulders and yawned. 'Cracking an axe into solid ice certainly uses up excess energy; you should try it.'

Suddenly, she hated him. He must know how she had fought to convince herself that it would be wrong to sleep with him, must know she had waited for him half the night, half hoping, half fearing, that he would come to her. She turned away from him, examining with spurious interest the nautical books on his shelf.

'I don't suffer from excess energy, sir. Or not the sort that can only be appeased by ice-breaking, or s-sex.'

'You damned little liar!' He grabbed her, pulling her roughly on to his knees and before she could escape his hand slid straight up beneath her sweater and captured her breast. His words had been harsh, but his hand gentled her breast, and he pushed her back to lie in the curve of his other arm with firmness, not angrily. 'You want me every bit as much as I want you!'

His touch lit a flame in her and he knew it. He sank his mouth on to hers, kissing her fiercely, forcing her mouth into submission whilst his hand squeezed her breast and then slid down, pushing past the waistband of her old corduroy trousers, fondling the smooth flatness of her stomach. And all the while his mouth roused her, so that she began to respond with a fierceness which matched his and with a deepening delight.

One moment they were entwined, the next, it seemed, she had landed on the floor. Alone. She sat up, dazed, her body still wanting him. He was standing at the voice pipe in the corner of the cabin, shouting orders, then turning towards her, urgency in the way he stood, his voice and face.

'Oh, my love! On the bridge, pronto!'

She got to her feet somehow and pulled her sweaters, inexplicably up round her armpits, down into their proper position. Had he called her his love? She touched her mouth, knowing it swollen from his kisses. How could she go up to the bridge looking like this? She glanced into his small mirror and saw herself, pupils enlarged by sensation, cheeks pink, hair tousled. She touched her mouth again. It looked...kissed.

He was struggling into his boots, then he reached out and grabbed her hand.

'Come on. Oh!' He had noticed her mouth. He reached into his locker drawer and drew out a mint lump. He grinned, a flash of white teeth in his dark face. 'Chew it slowly!'

She popped the mint into her mouth, appreciating that it would hide the state of her lips, then as they emerged into the corridor, tugged at his sleeve.

'Why the bridge, Skipper?'

'We've found a shoal so we're going to shoot the trawl.'

'And...the ice?'

He glanced down at her, his expression veiled.

'We used the steam hoses last night as well as axes. It's no longer a danger to stability.'

'Oh!' She was shocked to realise that her feelings were mixed. She said quickly, before he noticed the pause, 'That's wonderful. I really didn't want to be another statistic in police records—you know the sort, young girl disappears without trace.'

He gripped her wrist for a moment, then released it.

"The grave's a fine and private place.
But none, I think, do there embrace."

'Marvel put it in a nutshell, didn't he!' He paused, looking down at her with an odd expression on his face. 'Know the rest of that poem?'

She shook her head.

'Well, some day, when this little lot's over, I'll recite it to you!'

They entered the bridge then, and routine took over, allowing her no time for questioning. Except that, over and over, the words "my love", sang in her head.

They fished for three days and three nights, and only stopped because the captain knew the deckhands had to have a break. The catches were all good, the fishrooms were filling up, the men beginning to murmur about home. Yet still they pressed on further north.

'Suppose we tow on the way home? We could complete our catch then. No need to steam further north because it's all ground that has to be retraced, with winter deepening all the time, and the ice liable to trap our retreat.'

That was the mate, as the officers sat around their dining table eating roast beef. The captain took a big mouthful and seemed to consider as he chewed. Then he spoke.

'We'll press on for a bit yet.'

In the mess deck there was open rebellion. They understood his hunger for the fish but it was madness to continue to steam north, they told each other. The ship was low in the water with the weight of the catch and from the leaks, ill-equipped to match storm conditions, with the speed and buoyancy so necessary. Any hour might bring another blizzard, a couple of freak waves, a berg which could cripple them. It was madness!

Chuffy was pale, his leg painful. He needed to exercise it gently, but in the constant motion of the heaving seas this was impossible.

He needed to see a doctor too, Frankie knew, because he had a racking cough still, and though he was much better, he wheezed when he moved. She had grown fond of her patient and it was for his sake, in the end, that she approached the captain.

He was on the bridge. He face was drawn, his expression harsh, but she did not hesitate.

'Captain? Can I speak to you?'

He nodded. They were alone on the bridge.

'Why won't you turn for home, sir?'

'Because I need another forty tons to make this a record catch.'

She took a deep breath and moved nearer to him, looking up into his face.

'Skipper, Chuffy needs to get home! We've done our best, but he should see a proper doctor. Won't you turn back?'

He shook his head impatiently, frowning down at her.

'No! I told you, we need another forty tons.'

'Will you turn back if I...' her voice faltered then strengthened again. 'If I come to your cabin?'

There was a long silence. She felt the blood drain from her face. Then she opened her eyes and looked up at him. His face was grimmer than she had ever seen it.

'Are you offering to be my mistress?'

She nodded; opened her mouth, closed it

again. There seemed nothing further to say.

He turned back to the wheel, away from her.

'No. We'll go north.'

His tone brooked no argument, not that she would have attempted any. She felt deeper humiliation than she had ever imagined it possible to feel. She had offered herself to this man and he had scorned her. Mercilessly, without even the softening note of an explanation.

She turned away without another word and left the bridge. He would never come to her now. He had wanted her once and wanted her no longer. It was as simple as that.

An hour later they shot the trawl and when they hauled, brought up the biggest and best catch they had taken so far. Fishing continued all that night and until late the next day. Weariness seemed a part of them all, for Frankie worked shift for shift with the men. It was better than lying in her own cabin, unable to sleep, her mind sore and sick.

When the trawl came up at ten o'clock that night and spilled the huge cod down into the pounds, the skipper shot up the bridge window and leaned out.

'Lash the trawl, Wally. We're heading home.'

They were too tired to cheer, but from her position in the bridge window, Frankie saw their faces light up as they stumbled from the deck. She knew her own face should have lit up too, for now Chuffy would get back sooner and would be seen by a proper doctor. But she was too tired and, flatly, she knew that the reprieve had come too late for her self-respect. All she wanted to do was to collapse into her bunk and sleep and sleep.

Later, she would face the homecoming. The emptiness of her life when the *Artic Glow* was no longer part of it. But for now, sleep and the brief forgetfulness it would bring was the only anodyne for her pain.

Two men were left on watch, sparks and the bosun, and the rest of the crew slept for twelve hours. When they awoke, the news had truly sunk in. They were steaming south!

10

It was strange, steaming south. Strange to know that whatever the echo sounder showed on the ocean bed there was no point in shooting the trawl. The fishrooms were laden with best quality cod, haddock and halibut and the crew could relax at last.

Taffy cooked huge and wonderful meals, bottles of rum and brandy mysteriously appeared and were handed round and Frankie almost enjoyed the days as they passed. She cooked, served and waited at table and knew herself drained, as if so much emotion had been unleashed in the great cold and dark that she had none to spare for these milder seas. There was pain, of course, when the skipper spoke to her or touched her. He would touch her shoulder to get her attention, bend over the radio when she was listening in, his breath warm on her face. But after the sharpness of the agony she had felt when he had rejected her offer, the pain of mere indifference was dull.

The Captain was being circumspect, too. They were never alone save for when she took hot drinks to his cabin and then he would take the mug and tell her, brusquely, to leave. Though with the rest of the crew he was noticeably more relaxed and human.

'It's the smell of land coming close, see?' Taffy remarked one day as they were preparing dinner. 'He's not been to sea for a while so it got out of his system and things got him down, but now he can smell land and he's taking his responsibilities more lightly, like.'

'I thought he was the mate, acting skipper because the real one didn't turn up. Why did you say he'd not been to sea for a while?'

Taffy's eyebrows shot up.

'Whatever give you that idea? No, the gaffer stepped into the breach, like, when old Meadowes retired.'

'Oh.' Frankie left it at that. No point in discussing the skipper because very soon now, she would be leaving trawling for ever. The deckies had made a rough guess at their percentage and she knew that the money she received would be enough to see her through until she got another job. I shan't be a two-day millionaire, spending like mad and then signing on again, she thought wryly.

But when the *Artic Glow* sailed again, would there be a small figure on the quay, waiting for one last glimpse of the ship and her skipper? It would be madness, but she knew she would do it.

195

'Come on now, lad, take the officers their grub!'

Roused from her reverie, Frankie picked up the heavy dish and set off for the dining cabin.

'Skipper, I've been detailed to clean the bridge. I want to get the carpet cleaned.'

Frankie, with the rest of the crew, was polishing and repairing the *Artic Glow* until no one could have guessed at the hardships she had suffered in Arctic waters. But the captain was standing right in the middle of the bridge carpet, and she could scarcely tug it out from under his boots!

'Go ahead. What's holding you up?' He looked across at her, one brow climbing.

'You're standing on it, sir, I want it out on deck.'

He grinned but moved away and when she returned, with the carpet clean and most of the dirt now adhering to herself, he had gone.

Cleaning everything up made her realise how dirty and neglected everything had begun to look after more than three weeks at sea, but at last she could stand back and view her handiwork with satisfaction. The bridge shone.

Returning to the galley, where Taffy was painting the overhead pipes, she asked for another task. Taffy scratched his head with the brush handle and considered.

'Yes, make two plates of sandwiches, and take 'em along to the cabin and the mess deck. Coffee, too. I've let the fire out and I don't want to mess about with no cooking.'

She left the officers' sandwiches in their cabin, then went to the mess deck. Only Chuffy, still on light duties because of his leg injury, was there. She passed him corned beef sandwiches and pickles, poured two mugs of coffee, then sat down, glad to rest for a moment.

'Soon be home, Chuffy. How's the leg?'

'Fine. Good job, it's the party tonight.' He took a large mouthful of sandwich and spoke thickly through it. 'You'd better steer clear. It can get rough.'

'I can cope.'

Chuffy stared for a moment, then leaned over and patted her cheek.

'You've grown up! When you first came aboard you were just a kid, but I reckon you're right. You can cope with most things now.'

So party-time found her on the mess deck, looking with awe at the assortment of bottles on the tables. There was rum, brandy, whisky, beside more exotic things. The men were sitting round ready to start drinking and Jammy grinned across the table at her.

'With the officers' compliments, tiddler,' he said, waving towards the bottles. 'A tot for you, two tots for me, and the rest for these boozy blighters.'

'A tot? Oh, I can take more than that!'

But it was strong stuff to a young stomach unused to alcohol, and after sampling three tots, Frankie felt very happy indeed. Chuffy, noticing, spoke with some concern.

'Watch it, young 'un; you'll be stripping off and dancing on the table in a moment.'

Frankie peered at him.

'I'm all right. Chuffy, why are there two of you?'

Jammy, sitting beside her, chortled.

'The tiddler's gone got himself squiffy!'

'I am not!' Frankie sat up straight. 'I'm right all quite!'

'I say!' Jammy nudged her. 'You're not squiffy, you're nissed as a pewt!'

Frankie sniffed and seized the bottle to pour herself another dram. Jammy laughed at her, but she warded him off, tipped the drink and down her throat and blinked as it seemed to explode in her stomach.

'I feel great! I feel...I feel...'

Jammy, watching sympathetically, saw her face change to a pale shade of green even as the captain entered the mess deck. He was holding the tally in one hand.

'Want to know what you're celebrating, lads?' He waved the tally. 'You're celebrating a catch of 130 tons of fish, which is a record. The old *Artic Glow*'s never taken such a catch since the day she was launched.'

The cheers seemed to rock the mess deck and Frankie got to her feet. If she didn't get some fresh air she would throw up! Somehow, she reached the corridor and stood swaying, the shiny floor in front of her a mute reproach. Was she going to sully its freshness?

She was. The skipper, emerging from the mess deck, found her prostrate and still heaving and carried her, empty and reeking, along to the shower cubicles.

He held her head under the cold water, then allowed her to stand clear and eye him defiantly. He was not, however, furious with her but almost amused.

'Better? A bad time to take to drink when my ship's nice and clean!'

'I'm all right now.'

He eyed her quizzically.

'I can't say you look it! Well, clean up the mess you've made, and then straight to bed, I think.'

She obeyed him, then tumbled into her bunk and slept deeply, only rousing when the crew turned in. They appeared to have a fight right outside her door, but it was probably merely a rowdy and boozy goodnight.

She smiled to herself and dropped back to sleep.

The last day dawned. By tea-time they were within sight of the docks. The men were in their shoregoing best and Frankie blinked at so much colour. But not even the shiny blue suits and vivid ties could hide their strength, their ruggedness.

They made their way through the lock gates to No. I Dock ahead of the fleet, which would improve their prices. The men were shouting as the ship was tied up, lugging their suitcases down on to the quayside, joking, threatening.

Frankie said her goodbyes and then went to the galley. Taffy was putting the fire out so that, when the ship was ready to sail once more, it would be a simple matter to light it again.

'Hi, Taff. Still not gone, then?'

'Always last to leave, me and the skipper. It'll be a while before the ship signs on again with a holed hull, she'll be in dry dock for a few weeks. Sign on together, shall we? You come round my lodgings, we'll talk it over.'

'I'll come round.' She picked up the small canvas bag she had acquired and smiled at the cook. 'Bye, Taff.'

'See you, tiddler. Be good!'

Full darkness had fallen when she reached the deck. It seemed right that she should leave now, say farewell to the ship which had taken her into day-long dark and taught her so much. She walked across the deck, slippery with the light, misty rain that was falling. It had been an unforgettable experience, she must cling to that thought when all else failed her.

'Hey!'

She turned. The skipper was leaning out of the bridge window, beckoning. She raised her eyebrows.

'Yes, sir?'

'Here!'

She went in by the bridge door and stood inside, staring across at him. Soft, dark hair flopped across his brow, his hard gray eyes were steady from staring into darkness and blizzards. A man immeasurably strong. She marvelled at her own temerity in refusing him anything, but she had found the strength to do so and it was useless to regret it now.

'Well, tiddler? It's all over. Come here.'

She went towards him and his arms came round her, pulling her closer yet. She stood stiff and motionless between his hands. She could *not* say goodbye or she would start to cry, and...

'What, no goodbye kiss? Oh, Frankie, my own love!'

She held aloof a moment longer, then crumpled against him, clutching his jersey, weeping into the hollow of his shoulder.

'Why do you call me that? You don't mean it!'

He was holding her so close now that she could feel his heartbeat thundering against her small breasts.

'I do mean it! I wanted you from the first moment I found you were a girl. Dammit, didn't I say so?'

'Oh, want! That's not love!'

'Lust and love are poles apart, eh?' He laughed and bent his head, kissing her eyelids, her tear-wet cheeks. 'When a man lusts after a woman's body, yet loves her with his whole heart, that's really something. I could have taken you, my darling, and it would have been wrong. Damn it, you were in my power and in my charge! I wanted us to make love from mutual desire and need, not because I was your boss and could dictate your actions! Isn't there something you want to tell me?'

His voice, she thought, sounded almost wistful.

'Skipper, you *know* I love you! I didn't offer to sleep with you just for Chuffy's health, and I wanted to die when you turned me down.'

'Damn it, Frankie, what sort of a bloke

202

would agree to a deal like that? Turn back and you can have me!'

Frankie laughed, seeing his point of view for the first time.

'When you put it like that...I tried to hide it, but you must have guessed I wanted you every bit as much as you wanted me!'

'I did have an inkling.' He kissed her and their mutual longing fused on the kiss, his hands pressing into the small of her back, arching her hard against him.

The opening of the bridge door went unnoticed; Taffy had to cough before they broke apart. And then not far apart. Over the top of Frankie's head, the skipper raised questioning brows.

'Sorry, sir, I didn't realise you'd got a...a visitor.' In the dimness of the unlit bridge Taffy's eyes wandered curiously over the girl's slim figure as she clung to the captain. 'I came to ask if you'd like a little something, but I see you've got it already!'

He chuckled at his own joke and then, as the skipper continued to regard him silently, jerked his hand in a half salute and left the bridge, closing the door softly behind him.

The skipper sighed and put Frankie gently back from him.

'Taffy didn't know you. What about that?'

'I've stopped pretending to be a boy, that's

why. Sir, when we're married can I sail with the *Artic Glow?*'

He laughed, then sat down in the leather swivel chair in front of the radio and pulled her on to his lap.

'Certainly not! For one thing, I'm going to promote Len to skipper the *Artic Glow*. He'll make a first-rate captain.'

'Then you'll be out of work!'

He turned her in his arm so that he could see her face. It was pale and tear-streaked, and the most beautiful face he had ever seen.

'My love, have you ever heard me referred to as the gaffer?'

'Of course. And the boss, the old man, all sorts. So what?'

He hugged her, then rested his chin on the top of her head.

'I'm the owner, Frankie. My father was a fleet owner and he believed men should start from the bottom in trawling—it's a tough game. I worked my way up, got my master's ticket, and when my father died, I went ashore to run the business. I took over when Meadowes left because the men were saying the *Artic Glow* was an unlucky ship. I'd not been to sea for eight or nine years, but I wanted to prove them wrong. And did. Now I'll go back ashore again, manoeuvring stocks and shares instead of trawling the seas. Do you still want to marry me?'

'Then you won't go away and leave me behind?' Frankie snatched up his hand and bit the knuckles hard, to mark. 'If you knew! I w-wished myself dead! All that danger—and I thought you just wanted me to take your mind off the risks!'

'I won't go away. Or I might, if you bite like that often! I must say it didn't occur to me, but I suppose the reverse. could be true. You might only want *me* to take your mind off the dangers!'

'No! I want you all the time, I...' she saw the twinkle in his eyes and pouted. 'Well, I don't care if you think I'm a brazen hussy! I am brazen now!'

She turned in his arms, pulling his head down to hers. His hands caressed her, trembling against her cool, bare skin beneath the rough jersey.

'Oh Frankie, my own love!'

Taffy, making his way across the deck, glanced towards the bridge and saw them, entwined in the blue leather chair, absorbed in each other. It crossed his mind as he reached the quayside that the captain's girl bore a remarkable resemblance to his erstwhile galley boy. A sister, perhaps? He glanced back once more, but they had disappeared. In the faint light the chair rocked, empty.

Taffy grinned to himself and hurried towards the beckoning lights of the pubs in Freeman Street. Whatever the skipper was doing, he hoped he was enjoying it. After the sort of trip they had had, they all deserved some relaxation!

And Frankie, responding ardently to her lover's touch, suddenly thought of something.

'Skipper, do you realise I don't even know your name!'